Marley Parker
A Rumor of Ghosts

Maria Sigle

Also by **Maria Sigle**

Marley Parker

To Jill—
Thank you such for
your support and friendship!
I think you are beautiful
inside and out.
Much love,
Maria
xx

Praise for Marley Parker

“Move over Nancy Drew. There’s another attractive young gal sleuthing on the block—Marley Parker, courtesy of an exciting new author, Maria Sigle. Marley, a county sheriff’s daughter dead set on becoming an investigative journalist, is on the trail of the murderer of a wealthy college dean. Like Nancy, Marley’s got it all, but it almost comes to naught in a spine tingling wind-up to a well crafted mystery.”

-TAYLOR PENSONEAU, *Author of Brothers Notorious & The Summer of ‘50*

“Marley Parker keeps the reader guessing from one chapter to the next, and delivers a surprise ending that neatly ties everything together in an unexpected way. One of the most interesting aspects of the main character is her devotion to her family. Marley Parker is no lone sleuth—she frequently helps (and is helped by) her father, Sheriff Parker, and her sister Jade. In one chapter, Marley takes a break from the main mystery to help discover who is stealing personal items from the girls’ locker room in her sister’s private high school, putting herself in harm’s way in the process.

-MICHAEL KLEEN, Author of *Haunting Illinois & Founder of Mysteriousheartland.com*

This is a work of fiction. Names, characters, places, and incidents are either the product of the author's imagination or are used fictitiously, and any resemblance to any persons, living or dead, business establishments, events, or locales is entirely coincidental.

Marley Parker A Rumor of Ghosts

Mystery Girl Publishing

ISBN-13:
978-0692406861 (Mystery Girl Publishing)

ISBN-10:
0692406867

Acknowledgments

Thank you, Mary Schackmann, for all of your awesome help and ideas with my books. I'm lucky to have such a literary genius on my team.

A very special thank you to 'Doc' himself, Dr. Ron Havens—not only my favorite Psychology Professor, but everyone else's favorite as well. Thank you for inspiring me.

Thank you, Tom Gaskins/ Gaskins Designs, for once again designing such an amazing cover and for your willingness to always help a friend.

Thank you to Chad Mitchell Photography for the use of your beautiful photographic artistry and always making me look good.

I would not be able to write any books at all without the support of my family members, many of whom have inspired some of my favorite characters. Always first in my book are my children, Johnny and Jordan, and of course, my husband, John Sigle, the best damn foot surgeon in the country.

To my parents, Tony and Ann Libri, my in-laws, John & Kathy Sigle, my Grandma, Maryann (Reents) Martin, the picture of strength and beauty: Thank you for always supporting me, no matter what, 'A bushel and a peck.' I started off with one sister, but later on, God blessed me with two more. They are all extraordinarily different from each other but each capture parts of my heart in such different ways. Emily, Kara, and Isabella, you are all exceptional in your own ways. My Grandma ('Grannie Annie') Ann Libri, the most fun person I will ever know: Thank you for all of the laughs and always looking to the bright side of things. I love you.

Thank you, Mom, Donna (Martin) Libri, my guardian angel and my inspiration. You brought faith and joy into the lives of everyone you ever met.

In loving memory of my great Uncle, Bob Reents: You were a blessing to everyone who knew you.

Check out** www.marleyparker.com **for discount codes, author updates, photos, upcoming book-signing dates, and book club guides. Look for the third book in the Marley Parker series, 'Redletter.' Available from Mystery Girl Publishing in 2016.

“Hope is the thing with feathers that perches in the soul, and sings the tune without the words, and never stops at all.”

EMILY DICKINSON, "Hope is the thing with feathers"

For Emily & Phil Wetherell

PROLOGUE

I walked out into the brisk autumn evening, pulling my pashmina tighter around me. I looked up at the stars, to see an expansive moon hung low in the sky. It was quiet, peaceful. I forced myself to look forward and not back toward the hotel to see if he was coming after me. Hastily, I picked up my pace until I broke out into a run. I must have looked incredibly ridiculous as I sprinted through the vast parking lot in my five-inch heels and evening gown, but what did I care? Never again would I fall for his charm, his magnetic pull that had sucked me in deeper with each kiss. I felt so incredibly stupid.

Without warning, hot tears stung my eyes and rolled down my pale face. I unlocked my car and conscientiously climbed in, careful not to rip the delicate white fabric on the designer dress—the gift that I should never have accepted. It was a beautiful, shining symbol of a relationship that was doomed from the start, another lapse in judgment from the trusting, naïve Marley.

I turned the key in the ignition and a familiar old rock song blared powerfully from the speakers, something about a *'stranglehold.'* I didn't care; it helped drown out my steady stream of despondent thoughts. I glanced in the rearview mirror and used the back of my hands to wipe away the dripping streaks of black mascara. I pushed a button that lowered the heavy convertible top, that's when I saw *it*. The white envelope, with my name written across the middle in a meticulous script.

I sat frozen in my seat for a moment, just staring at it. Unsure I wanted to see what was inside. Slowly, I put the car back into park, opened my door, and carefully plucked out the envelope. Fearful of whatever lies and excuses I was about to endure, I tore open the envelope, slowly unfolded the letter and began to read the carefully typed script.

'Blood is red.

Veins are blue.

The bottom of the lake is where they will find you.'

CHAPTER 1

It all started with a leaky faucet. So I'll start there. I woke up to find a growing puddle of water lying in the middle of my bathroom floor. Rather than call a plumber, I thought it would be best to call Wayne first. Wayne is my Uncle and wayward landlord, who was currently gallivanting around Tuscany with his newest wife, Heather. I was slightly taken aback when he instructed me to go knock on my neighbor's door and ask him to take a look at my leaky pipes.

"You want me to do what?" I used my shoulder to prop my cell against my ear as I soaked up the water with old bath towels.

"Just walk over to Ryan's; he's the house directly next door. I think its number 7."

"Ryan?"

"Yeah, Ryan Duff."

"Seriously, Uncle Wayne? You want me to just go knock on the door of the biggest house on the lake and ask the owner to fix my leaky pipes?"

"What are ya, chicken?" he asked rhetorically. I overheard a woman's voice in the background ordering a glass of Chardonnay. I rolled my eyes. I could picture my Uncle Wayne as he spoke, with his long, thin frame casually outfitted in faded blue jeans, a well-worn t-shirt and cowboy boots, the dark sunglasses cleverly concealing the deep crows-feet that had begun to stretch further down his face with each passing year. He had a tendency to slowly run his fingers through his naturally sun-streaked blonde hair as he spoke—a habit he's had as long as I've known him. I imagined him sitting at a small private table for two, sipping wine with his new arm candy. He had a laid back way about him. His voice carried the same deep and steady cadence that used to lull me to sleep as a child.

"Ryan's my buddy," Uncle Wayne explained. "He's a plumber by trade. Great guy," he added emphatically. "He can fix anything. That's how he started his company, by fixing leaky faucets. Now he owns Ryan Duff Plumbing or 'R.D.P.' for short. It's the fastest growing plumbing company in the country. The guy's a genius. Why don't I just give him a call for you?"

"Thank you. That would probably be best. How's Italy?"

"Bellissimo! We should plan a family trip out here soon. You would love it."

We said our goodbyes and it seemed like before I could even finish drying off the floor, there was a knock at my front door. I answered hastily, tripping over the mat that lay in front of the door, to find a tall drink of water standing on my front porch, holding a tool box in one hand and what appeared to be a pile of processed meat sticks in the other. He was either a strip-o-gram or Ryan Duff, the genius plumber.

"Heard ya got a leak," the tall, dark stranger said, in a brusque tone. He was attractive, with his shaved head and towering height. He must have been at least 6'4 or 6'5. His shaved head caused me to believe that he was prematurely going bald and had decided to make a preemptive strike by shaving the remaining hair off, rather than live with a cul-de-sac on top of his head. I placed him to be somewhere in his mid-forties.

"You must be Ryan. Thanks for making it over so fast." I found it impossible to hide the pleasure I derived from his hasty arrival to my damsel-in-distress call.

"No problem. I was just on my way to the office when Wayne called." He showed himself into my house with the cocky assurance of a self-made man. I got the impression he was on a tight schedule and seemed already to know the exact location of the bathroom

"I take it you've been here before?" I asked curiously.

"Once or twice, when your Uncle first bought the place. He still living in Seattle?" he asked, with a sort of amused tone, like he knew something that I didn't about my Uncle's living situation.

"Yep. I don't get to see him very often, unfortunately."

Ryan didn't hesitate before plopping his body down on the bathroom floor. His longs legs practically reached the hallway as he lay on his back to examine the inner workings of my sink. "I almost forgot. These are for you," he said, as he presented me with the stack of individually packaged meat sticks, as if he was handing me a bouquet of flowers.

I looked down at him curiously.

"Deer jerky. Made it myself from my first ten point buck of the season," he said, with a look of pride.

"Oh, uh . . . thank you. I've never had deer jerky before." I tried my best to sound grateful, even though my stomach gave an involuntary flip. I carried a deep disdain for any type of meat stick, Buffalo wing, or any other carnival type of meat. I think it had something to do with my childhood. Growing up without a mother, my sister and I had to eat whatever my dad, the bachelor, was cooking—which, on any given night, was typically Buffalo wings.

With quick, fluid motions he began working with ease, twisting and unscrewing pipes as he removed something disgusting from the drain and tossed it into the trash can, without giving it a second thought.

I was impressed with the way he made conversation as he worked—almost like the work at hand was an afterthought, something he could do blindfolded. His voice carried a hint of a small town twang and I noticed he was wearing a pair of worn-in cowboy boots.

We made small talk as he worked. Over the next fifteen minutes, small talk morphed into more personal talk. I asked how he'd gone from a small-town plumber to founding one of the nation's most successful plumbing companies and he asked me what it was like to bite someone's nose off.

Clearly, he had read my article in the Greenbriar Daily about my first case, my first-hand account of the murder of Robert Cummings, the Dean of Students at my college, Greenbriar University. When I discovered that the Mayor of Greenbriar was responsible for the Dean's death, it had made front page news. When I bit off his nose in self-defense and discovered that both Mayor Brackett and Dean Cummings were responsible for my mother's death back in 1996, it took my newfound stardom to a whole other level. We're talking national news; the press loved the story. Nancy Grace discussed it for three nights in a row and interviewed me over the phone.

"This shouldn't give you any more trouble," Ryan said, as he sat up and wiped his hands off on his jeans before gathering his things. He had mastered the art of remaining modest while exuding exceptional confidence at the same time.

I saw Ryan out after thanking him profusely. He suggested that we get together for a neighborly cookout sometime soon and insisted I call him if I ever needed anything. He stressed the word *anything.*

I thought about Ryan for a moment after he left. I wasn't sure what to think. My gut told me that he was a good guy. However, the rumors I'd heard suggested otherwise. He seemed solid. Smart. Crazy smart, in fact, but not overtly intelligent. He kept it under wraps. I had heard from the small town rumor mill that he was a player, loose with his money and his morals. I decided, a long time ago, never to judge anyone based on other opinions or gossip. In fact, when I thought about the rumors about Ryan, they didn't match up to the Ryan that had just been in my house. I had a feeling jealousy was a major motivator behind the petty gossip—as it usually was in these cases. I would be lying if I said my curiosity wasn't piqued.

Before heading out the door, I grabbed a banana and gave my appearance a quick check in the mirror. I chose a pair of indigo-washed skinny jeans and my favorite jacket: black vegan leather.

CHAPTER 2

After I finished up my morning classes, I walked across campus to meet my new friend, the psychic and famous Criminal Psychologist, Dr. Cat Hopkins. I told her I'd stop by her office and we could drive to our little afternoon outing together. She had agreed to have lunch with me at 'Pirates' Cove' restaurant, tucked discreetly into the first floor of the 'Brass Lantern Inn' hotel.

The owner of the hotel, Glen McGuire, had hired me to investigate rumored hauntings in his establishment. The Brass Lantern Inn was one of Greenbriar's best known historical sites and recently Glen had encountered some paranormal activity. Understandably freaked out, he was hoping I might be able to at least look into it and with any luck come up with some sort of remedy. I decided it would be a good idea to bring Cat along, not only for moral support but also because she claims to have ESP. I thought it was a joke too, until her 'powers,' for lack of a better term, actually saved my life.

I walked over to the building that housed the Psychology department where Cat's office was located. I took in the sights and sounds of autumn all around me. It was a bright sunny day, with a steady mild breeze that caused the leaves to rattle around on the ground. It was October and officially Fall in Greenbriar—although, at this time of year, the locals referred to their hometown as 'Screambriar,' the reason being that everyone in town took Halloween very seriously. In fact, it was downright obnoxious. From the first day of October to the last, there were constantly events commemorating the only day of the year where the dead roam freely among the living. From Corn Mazes, Haunted Hayrides, an excess of haunted houses, and caramel apple tastings to pumpkin carving contests and trick or treating, it was a non-stop windstorm of festive activities that didn't let up until November 1st.

A major reason for this was due to the fact that Greenbriar was rumored to be a popular home for witch covens in the late 1600s. Everyone knows about the Salem witch trials on the east coast, but what most people don't know is that Northern Illinois was loaded with haunted folklore and legendary ghost stories were rumored to have occurred right here, in this quaint Midwestern town. The stories were passed down for generations and tended to change a little with each telling, but the central story always remained the same. John and Eliza Bower had three children: two teenage daughters and a young son. The parents were accused of practicing witchcraft and the entire family was hanged and displayed in town. From that day forward, the fate of the Bower family served as a cautionary tale to those involved in any sort of black magic.

Aside from several infamous stories about witchcraft, there was also one about a headless horseman. Well, not *the* headless horseman from Irving's novel, about the Hessian soldier who had his head blown off by a stray cannon. This was a legend that locals referred to as the 'Yankee Horseman.' During the Civil War, a Yankee soldier was mistaken for a rebel soldier and was accidentally beheaded by his own people while riding his horse in battle, somewhere around the area of what is now Greenbriar. Illinois bordered on the edge of the Mason-Dixon Line that divided the Confederate states from the Union states. Because of that story, there was a bronzed statue in the middle of the downtown square: a brave union soldier in uniform riding his galloping horse and holding his head in his lap. Who was to say whether or not the legends were true? If nothing else, they served as an unearthly backdrop to the supernatural holiday.

Trick or treating was an event in and of itself. Instead of one night, the tricks and treats actually went on every night during the week of Halloween. From Monday all the way to Sunday, children had the chance to dress in costume and fill up their buckets with sugary sweets, seven nights in a row. Every house in town not only displayed cleverly carved jack-o'-lanterns but typically had ghosts and goblins lurking from every window, roof top and doorway. Locals went all out for Halloween the way most people go all out for Christmas.

"There she is. The talk of the town," said Doctor Will Warner, or 'Doc' as I lovingly referred to him. He was my favorite professor and mentor, although most students would say the same. He sat casually on the front of Cat's desk, cup of coffee in hand, wearing his habitual ensemble of a plaid sport coat, jeans, and red Converse sneakers. Cat was seated behind the desk, in the midst of gathering her things.

"Look at this, my two favorite professors in one room," I announced, always happy to see Doc and Cat. The two of them had met nearly twenty-five years ago, when the University was new; they were two of the longest tenured professors on campus and the most popular. The popularity was mostly a result of the national media attention they both received for their individual work and for advances in their respective fields. "Why don't you join us for lunch, Doc?"

"Good idea. Why don't you join us, Will? I'd like your take on the situation as well," Cat chimed in.

"I'm not exactly sure how much help I'll be. I'm neither a psychic nor a famous cub reporter, but what the hell?" Doc teased, before he flashed us a prominent devilish grin, the kind that always made it seem like he was secretly up to something.

When we were seated at the Pirates' Cove, I took a moment to study my surroundings. The restaurant was outfitted top to bottom with authentic-looking fisherman's décor that looked as if had actually come from an ancient pirate ship. Perhaps it was the dimly lit rooms and mossy stone covered walls that added to the overall effect. I had way too much nervous energy to eat, so I ordered a diet coke; despite protests from the two doctors in the room. While Doc ordered some sushi rolls, Cat decided on the catch of the day, which the menu indicated was a pan-seared red snapper with a champagne butter sauce. Just as we were finishing up, Glen McGuire, the owner of the hotel and restaurant, spotted us and approached our table.

"I hope you enjoyed everything. It's not every day we have local celebrities dining in our establishment." Glen spoke in his usual humble, reserved tone.

"Ha . . . celebrities? Hardly." Doc uttered a little chuckle and scratched his bald head.

"Speak for yourself, Doc," I teased, and gently elbowed him in the side. "So, Glen, I hope you don't mind. I brought along Dr. Cat Hopkins and Dr. Will Warner from Greenbriar University to help assist me with our investigation. Doc Warner is the head of the Journalism department and Cat is the head of the Psychology department and a psychic," I added proudly.

Doc choked on his iced tea and Cat blushed.

"I think what Miss Parker means is: I do have what some might call a sixth sense, if you will. I just don't go around advertising it," Cat replied, clearly caught off guard and perhaps a little irritated with my frankness.

"Oh, well, then . . . I think you came to the right place," Glen said. "The hotel has been losing business at a staggering rate. Any extra help you can offer would be greatly appreciated. Shall we get started?"

Glen led us through the restaurant and up the stairs, stopping at the third floor. The suites at the Brass Lantern Inn occupied the second and third floors. The floorboards were creaky and there was a faint underlying musty smell. The place instantly gave me the creeps and I subconsciously stepped in a little closer to Doc.

"So, this floor is probably where most of the . . . ahh . . . sightings—or whatever you want to call them—have taken place." Glen was clearly embarrassed by the mere mention of the scandalous topic at hand.

"Can you tell us what, *specifically,* you have seen or heard?" I asked skeptically, giving my best impersonation of a serious Journalist.

"I suppose, most of the time, it's a cold chill or perhaps a shadow out of the corner of your eye. Some guests have complained of things being moved around."

Cat immediately intercepted his train of thought. "Well, the cold chills are an extremely common sign of paranormal activity. Have you noticed any electrical problems?"

"Yes, actually." Glen furrowed his brow. "But the most alarming piece of evidence, I suppose, is the actual ghost itself."

"Come again?" Doc asked. He appeared to be suppressing a laugh. His rigorous education and training had taught him to be highly skeptical of such abnormal occurrences. *Everything can be explained in one way or another,* he would preach. *There is absolutely no such thing as the paranormal.* How he and Cat were such close friends was completely beyond me.

"I . . . I know how it sounds," Glen stammered. "But people have actually seen a full-on apparition . . . myself included. She makes herself known, whenever she feels like it, I suppose."

"She?" I asked, beginning to wonder if this man was indeed the nutter I had him pegged for.

"Addy," Glen said, in a matter of fact tone. "At least, that's what she apparently told one of the guests. Here, I'll show you where some of the appearances have been." He led us down the narrow hallway, which was desperately in need of a fresh coat of paint and new carpet. A buzzing light fixture on the right gave a quick flicker and I jumped ever so slightly. Glen pulled out a skeleton key and unlocked a room labeled number 309. The room was quaint, with lace curtains and cream colored satin bedding. The floral wall paper and old fixtures made it feel dated and in need of a more modernized feel. Needless to say, it was eerie.

As I entered the room and was immediately assaulted by a rush of arctic air. A woman's voice spoke directly into my right ear, so close it was almost as if she were on top of me, as she whispered, "Can't Breathe!"

"Whoa . . . What in the *hell* was that?" I addressed everyone else in the room with a look of shock.

Doc and Glen stared back at me blankly. Cat, on the other hand, shared the same expression of shock on her face. "I heard it too. '*Can't Breathe*'; it was as clear as day," she said reassuringly. "She was trying to get your attention, Marley. Maybe to warn you about something? I don't know, exactly."

Our revelation was abruptly interrupted by a shrill ring tone, which seemed to be coming from Doc's cell.

"This is Will Warner." Doc always answered his phone with the frankness of a seasoned journalist, never wanting to miss what could potentially be the lead for his next story or a source returning his call.

"What?" Doc's tone suddenly changed to anxious and borderline angry. "Wait for me. I'll be right there . . . ten minutes," he barked, completely out of character for him. His face turned pale, as if he was the one who had just heard the ghost.

"That was Max from campus police," he explained. "Rose . . . my assistant . . . she . . . she was attacked." He rubbed his forehead; his fingertips left red streaks on his pale skin. "She's in a coma."

CHAPTER 3

We pulled back into campus at a formidable speed, my encounter with Addy's ghost now seeming trivial—silly, even—in light of the devastating news that was just received. Rose's life was on the line.

Rose Daily was a new friend of mine. She was a waitress at Dean Robert Cummings's home, Manor Hill Estate. She was the one responsible for switching my poisonous bowl of soup with Dean Cummings's non-poisonous bowl, which, in turn, saved my life. I would be forever indebted to Rose, even though I never did find out exactly why she switched those bowls. It's a fact that continues to haunt me, even in my sleep. She was also Doc Warner's new Teaching Assistant. Sweet, shy, demure Rose. From what I knew, I didn't think she had any family here. She didn't have many friends, not that I knew of anyway. I still didn't know all that much about her. She was a Journalism major as well.

Somehow, the thought of Rose as a Journalist always struck me as odd. It was an ill-suited profession for someone who seemed to shy away from most people. She was low-key. She preferred to stay behind the scenes, blend in, and keep to herself. I couldn't see her hiding out in the hills of Afghanistan, wearing a Middle Eastern hijab and waiting to report on enemy ceasefire, or initiating groundbreaking interviews with a Cuban dictator or the leader of North Korea. At any rate, it didn't matter right now. The only thing that mattered was her health and figuring out who her attacker was. I had to get to the bottom of this and find out exactly who attacked Rose and why. I'd worry about exacting my revenge once all of that was finalized. Whoever did this would not get away with it. I would personally see to that.

We pulled into the campus police station—all three of us on a mission to find out precisely the events as they unfolded and anything further about Rose's condition. The campus officer on the scene was Max Cooper, who preferred to be called 'Coop.' He had a rather jovial disposition given what had just happened, which stuck in my craw. Apparently, Officer Cooper was the one who had come to Rose's aid and called for an ambulance.

"What exactly do we know?" Cat was nothing if not direct. No time wasted on the art of small talk, just the facts.

"Well . . . I saw this old grey Honda illegally parked over there, on the side of the road, over by the soccer fields." Officer Coop pointed in the general direction of nothing exactly. I found the slowness with which he spoke to be highly irritating. " . . . The hazard lights were flashing, which seemed strange to me. So, then I decided to take a closer look, and wouldn't ya know it? There's a girl lying in the grass. She was all covered in blood and bruises. Clothes ripped. Unresponsive. Nothing like I had ever come across before on one of my shifts." He crossed his arms in front of his body, staring off into the distance, reliving the memory. "I called for backup and told them to send an ambulance. I looked around the area. It was pretty quiet, ya know, being early in the morning. There's not a whole lot of action on campus, mid- morning. All the kids are already on campus and morning classes have already started. Anyhow, you would not believe all the blood—"

"Did you see anything or anyone out of the ordinary?" I cut him off before he could elaborate further on the gory state of my friend's condition.

"No, no. I didn't notice anything odd. Didn't see anyone fleeing the scene, if that's what you mean."

"Did you notice anything? Anything at all? Did you take a good look around?" I was at the end of my patience with this rent-a-cop.

"Hmmm...No. No, I did not. But there was a student who witnessed a man driving away from the scene. I'm sure it was probably nothing. I already let her go. I'm letting the authorities handle things from here on out."

Doc and I exchanged knowing glances.

I had to find this student. This witness. "What's the name of the witness?"

Officer Coop smiled in response, like I was trying to pull a fast one on him. "Now, I'm not allowed to—"

"First of all, wipe that smug grin off your face. My friend is lying on her death bed. If you don't tell me the name of this witness, I'll just ask my dad. Maybe you've heard of him, Sherriff Parker? He doesn't take too kindly to people disrespecting his daughter. Deal with me or deal with him." When it came to those I cared about, I was unstoppable.

Doc Warner immediately intervened, after shooting me an irritated glance. "I think what she means is . . . just help us out. Let us skip a step here and just give us the name of the witness. She's right . . . we will find out, but you could be a gentleman and save us a step. So tell me: What's the witness's name?" Doc Warner cleared his throat as he tried on bad ass for once. He wore it well.

Rent a cop 'Coop' rolled his eyes. "All I've got is a name." He hesitated. "Margaret Reynolds. Goes by Margie."

I spent the next twenty minutes or so in the library, trying to dig up contact info on Margaret Reynolds. I searched the internet and the student directory. Nothing. I could always take the easy way out and call my Dad, Madison County Sheriff, and have him look it up for me. Or even Matty, my dad's best friend and Deputy Sherriff, who had unlimited access to personal information on every county resident. Instead, I decided to sharpen my investigative reporting skills. After all, I wouldn't always be able to simply pick up the phone anytime I needed information. I had another idea. It was a long shot, but it might just work. I picked up my cell and punched in the phone number for the medical office on campus, as I slipped into the ladies room for privacy.

"Hello, this is Kelsey. How can I help you today?"

"Hi, Kelsey. This is Margie Reynolds. I just needed to double check my appointment time for my annual checkup. I lost my appointment card so I was hoping you look it up for me?"

"Of course, sweetie. How do you spell the last name?"

"R-E-Y-N-O-L-D-S." I spelled out the name and took a complete guess on the accuracy.

"Margaret Reynolds?"

"Uh, yes. That's me."

"I don't have anything in the computer for you, honey. Are you sure you made one?"

"Well, I thought I did, but I was in a hurry."

"When would you like to come in? I've got tomorrow afternoon at three o'clock?" she asked hopefully.

"Sure, that would be perfect. Could you tell me what contact information you have on file for me? I recently changed my cell number, so I just wanna make sure you have the right number on file." I held my breath. My fingers tightly gripped my pen as they hovered over my paper, prepared to write down the phone number. There was a long pause.

"Sorry about that. I had to put you on hold for a sec. Okay, looks like we have your cell number as 555-4908." Quickly, I scribbled down the info and hung up the phone as she was in the process of asking me the name of my health care provider. Before thinking it through, I dialed Margie's cell number. She picked up after the fourth ring.

"Hello," a rather sleepy female voice answered, giving me the impression that I had awakened her.

"Hi, Margie, my name is Marley Parker. I'm a close friend of Rose Daily's." There was a long pause on her end of the line and I could tell she was probably caught off guard. "The girl who was attacked on campus today," I reminded her.

"Oh, yeah. That chick was tore up. It was, like, I couldn't believe my eyes when I saw her just lying there."

"I know." I took a deep breath at the mere thought of it. "Look, I'm obviously not a cop. I'm just a friend of hers and I really want to help the police find who did this."

"Wait a minute. Did you just say your name is Marley Parker?" she asked rhetorically and cut me off before I could answer. "I know you! You're that bad ass chick who bit Mayor Brackett's nose off that everyone keeps talking about. That's so killer. Did Dean Cummings and Mayor Brackett really kill your mom?"

I tried not to let my emotions overtake me or get offended by her rude curiosity. "Yes, they really killed her. And I would bite his nose off again in a heartbeat, if given the chance. Probably even some other parts too."

"*Killer*." She sounded intrigued by me, in a creepy, gothic sort of way.

"I guess . . . You do what you have to, ya know?"

"Totally. We should like go out for drinks some night and you could give me all of the gory details. I play bass guitar in a band called the 'Crushed Skulls' at this club on campus—"

"Yeah, sure, that sounds like fun." I cut her off, unable to bear hearing any more about the crushed skulls, the band from hell. I pictured her with heavy black eye makeup, silver spikes through her nose and eyebrows, and about an extra ninety pounds of fat around her mid-section. "So, I was wondering if you wouldn't mind filling me in on what exactly you saw today."

"Oh, yeah . . . Sorry. Let me think . . . this morning . . . Yeah, I left my bag in class so I had to go back and get it, and on my way out of the building I noticed the grey car with the hazard lights on was still illegally parked, and then I saw some guy pulling away. He was driving some kind of official car. Undercover police car, maybe. It was a fairly new, white, four-door sedan—pretty sure it was a Ford. He had one of those removable sirens on top of his roof, though. Like one that you can take on and off."

"Did you get a plate number?"

"Are you for real? Why would I get the guy's plates?" Margie laughed facetiously to herself. "No, but I remember one thing, though. They were Indiana plates, *not* Illinois."

"Oh, good. That's something, Indiana plates. Well, is there anything else you recall? Even if you think it's nothing, it could prove to be significant later on."

"I only got a quick look at him. He gave me the creeps, though."

"What makes you say that?" I asked, my curiosity elevated.

"Something about the way he looked . . . the way he drove off. Like he wasn't in any hurry. He should have looked nervous or . . . or rushed to leave, but he just looked . . . calm. Almost cocky."

“Wait a minute, you saw his face? Did you get a good look?” I was shocked that she hadn’t revealed information like this sooner. This was a huge break.

“Yeah, I saw him. He was white, maybe late twenties or even early thirties.”

“And? Is that it? Do you remember anything more specific? Hair color? Eye color? Any distinguishing marks or tattoos?”

“No, I didn’t get a close enough look to see anything like that.” The tone in her voice was suddenly more pensive, as if she was in deep thought. “He just looked . . . creepy.”

CHAPTER 4

I didn't have enough time to swing by St. Aidan's Hospital to check on Rose, which probably didn't make much of a difference, seeing as though she was lying unconscious in the ICU and probably couldn't have visitors anyhow. I drove directly from campus to meet my sister Jade and her new boyfriend PJ. Jade and I attended Greenbriar's annual Halloween festival every year. It was probably the largest festival the town held, drawing residents from all over the state. People loved a good scare around this time of year and Greenbriar was full of them. The festival was held downtown and all the local businesses would decorate their storefronts and usually offered tricks and treats as well. Every year, the historic city hall was transformed into a haunted house by local city employees. It seemed to get more elaborate with each passing year.

The festival had a different theme each year and everyone came dressed in costume; this year's theme was 'Goth, Gore, & Horror.' I was expecting to see a lot of dark creatures with heavy makeup. I didn't have time to stop by the party store for a costume, so I was fated to stick out like a sore thumb in my short beige dress and five-inch heels. I grabbed my black vegan leather jacket from the back seat and threw it over my shoulders. There. That should help. The only other clothes I had available to change into were the previously worn, sweaty clothes from my gym bag. This would have to do. I pulled my red convertible into a vacant spot in front of the curb, touched up my lip-gloss, and fluffed out my hair with my fingertips.

The air was chilly; the scent of burnt leaves wafted in from somewhere in the nearby distance. I received a text from Jade, informing me that she and PJ were in front of the stage, waiting for me. I hurriedly trudged through the crowd, afraid of missing my dad give the opening speech and handing out the awards for best costumes. I pushed past the group of drunken frat boys dressed as skeletons, kids dressed up like their favorite superheroes with their buckets full of candy, and a lot of other scary gothic looking creatures. I ran into a teenage girl with fake blood covering her face and oozing from a prosthetic hanging eyeball. My stomach gave a lurch as I thought of Rose. I couldn't keep my mind off of her.

I accidentally bumped into a rather creepy looking man wearing heavy black eye liner, black lipstick, and an all-black pleather-looking ensemble.

"Excuse me. Sorry," I said in passing.

"Marley? Marley Parker?" the man in black asked. He studied me curiously, as if we knew each other. I briefly studied him but couldn't place him. His hair was died pitch black, to match his makeup, and around his neck he wore a dog collar with silver spikes. I couldn't tell if he was in costume or if this was his usual gothic garb. I continued to look at him blankly, without a clue who he was.

“Look at you, you little bunny. You haven’t changed since high school.”

I strained to hear him over the nearly deafening rock music that was being played by some local band. I only hoped that it wasn’t ‘*Crushed Skulls.’* They had just began playing their rendition of Michael Jacksons ‘Thriller,’ but the sounds were so jumbled it was hard to tell for sure. I studied the man in front of me, and for the life of me, I had absolutely no clue who he was.

“I’m sorry. I just don’t recognize—”

“It’s me, Larry Watson.” He cut me off, his black lips smiling expectantly. “Remember? We sat next to each other in Chemistry. You usually came in late and copied off my homework.”

“Oh my gosh! WEENIE?” I screamed over the music. “Is that really you? You’ve completely transformed yourself.” Sometimes blatant honesty was difficult to conceal; this was the perfect example.

“Yeah, well, no one has called me that since high school.” Ever so slightly taken aback by his old nickname, his churlish smile slowly dissipated and suddenly he was not quite as happy to see me.

“Oh, I’m sorry. I . . . ahh . . . verbal diarrhea. I’m sure that nickname has been long forgotten, Larry,” I lied. It was obvious that the mention of his old nickname had stunned and clearly offended him. My mind flashed back to images of the Larry Watson, better known as ‘Weenie,’ I’d known during our high school years. I’m pretty sure it was Jeff Staley, the quarterback of the football team, who’d dubbed Larry with the name Weenie after he had accidentally peed his pants during a pep rally in the gym. The name stuck with him all throughout high school. I never would have guessed in a million years that this dark creature with the spike through his tongue was little Weenie Watson. ''So, how are you? What are you doing with yourself these days?"

"I'm a ghost hunter. I started my own business, the 'Skeleton Crew'," Larry announced proudly.

It slowly began to dawn on me that his makeup and attire were probably not a costume at all.

"Ghost hunting? For real?" I asked, and feigned a smile, as I simultaneously tried to subdue my laughter. "Do you need a four year degree for that?" I asked rhetorically, and Weenie didn't laugh. "Seriously, can you actually, like, make a living off of that?"

"You'd be surprised just how busy we are," he said, as he dug into his jeans pocket. He removed a business card, which he flattened out before proudly presenting it to me. Weenie clearly took a great deal of pride in his eccentric profession, promoting himself as *the* authority on the nether world. He even dressed the part.

"Here ya go, check it out for yourself," Weenie added curtly, from behind his bruised ego. *What a jackass, his parents must be so proud of his career aspirations.* I glanced down at his card. It read 'Skeleton Crew' in bold print, with the words 'Serving Illinois and surrounding areas since 2013' in a smaller font. Underneath the print was a picture of Weenie staring into a massive crystal globe, as if he was searching for other-worldly answers.

Luckily, Jade had spotted me because I heard her calling my name from several feet away. "Gotta run! I'm meeting my sister. Thanks, for the card." I gave Weenie a little wave and smiled at him as I walked away, grateful to Jade for giving me a way out of the conversation. Once I was out of Weenie's eye sight, I tossed his business card into the closest trash bin, rolling my eyes as I caught another glimpse of his ridiculous picture.

"Hey! Marley!" my sister Jade called out from the front of the stage. I didn't recognize her at first; she was dressed head to toe in black plastic-like leather, with dark lipstick and heavy black eyeliner. I had forgotten that Jade told me she was dressing up as gothic-chic tonight. Whatever that meant.

"Laying it on a bit thick, aren't we?" I asked her, taken aback by the sex appeal her racy outfit exuded.

"If you ask me, Halloween's just an excuse for girls to dress up like whores," PJ offered. His costume was slightly more innocent than Jade's. Actually, I couldn't tell what exactly he was dressed as. At first sight, I thought he was an old lady, but upon closer inspection he appeared to be dressed as an enormous baby in a blue jumper, with a fake old lady in between his legs. It gave the illusion of a humongous baby sitting on a fragile old lady's back. He was wearing a matching blue bonnet and held onto an oversized baby bottle.

"Hello . . . the theme of the festival is Goth, Gore, and Horror," Jade teased him, with a fluttery bat of her eyelashes.

“Yeah, Horr-o-r.” PJ sounded out the word. “It starts with an H, not a W,” he said, grinning.

I couldn’t help but laugh. Jade’s new boyfriend was completely hilarious. He had a dry, razor sharp wit that kept everyone around him on their toes and kept Jade and me constantly laughing. He was an army brat and the youngest of six kids. His costume had no doubt been passed down to him by one of his many siblings. By the age of seven, he had lived in four different countries and had been home schooled for most of his life. His father, the Major General, had raised him to clean his plate, not to ask for anything, to believe that hard work was the only kind of work, and without fail to attend church every Sunday morning. It was his clean-cut, no nonsense approach that had made my dad approve of PJ dating his youngest daughter.

“You sound like my dad,” I yelled over the music. I noticed my Dad whom I lovingly refer to as ‘Tones’, making his way onto the stage; I couldn’t quite make out his costume. I took a few steps closer to the stage to get a better view.

“Welcome, citizens of *Screambriar,* to the 45th Annual Fright Fest!” He was wearing a black suit with a blue tie, and fake blood was smeared everywhere. There was a prosthetic nose, raw and bleeding, which dangled by some sort of plastic string from his face. He had two faux black eyes and wore a sign that read, “I got my ass kicked by a girl.” Obviously, he was dressed as the previous Mayor of Greenbriar, Tim Brackett, who was now rotting behind bars for life as he awaited his sentencing for a laundry list of criminal acts.

Most notably, these acts were the murder of Rob Cummings Senior, arson, and the hit and run of my Mother, Faith, nearly twenty years ago.

Tones began to tap his index finger impatiently on the microphone, checking to see if it was working, which it was, loud and clear. “How do you work this damn thing?” he asked no one in particular, clearly unaware whether or not it was turned on. “I’d like to ask my two beautiful daughters to come up on stage with me. For those of you who don’t know, these are my daughters, Jade and Marley.” He looked us up and down and frowned at our choice of attire, especially Jade’s, but continued on with his seemingly impromptu speech.

I looked around the crowd, searching for familiar faces. I recognized Mrs. Kingsdale, my fifth grade teacher, the creepy guy from the drycleaners, and Jeremy; the first boy I ever kissed. The costumes helped conceal everyone’s identity, but as I studied them, I saw a lot of people dressed up just like my Dad: the bloody bitten-off nose, black eyes, and suit with blood droplets scattered. I appreciated the fact that everyone found it so amusing, but it gave me the creeps. I’d been there. I’d lived it. I was the one who’d bitten Mayor Brackett’s nose off, in an attempt to save myself and Rob from ultimately being burned alive. The mere thought of it gave me the chills. I had to make myself stop remembering and plaster on a happy smile. I wasn’t over it. Maybe I never would be, but it was still too fresh in the forefront of my mind.

I felt like everything was happening so fast. Everything just started to spin. Rose had been beaten within an inch of her life; there was a madman on the loose around campus. I'd just had a rather creepy encounter with a ghost, and last but not least, Jade had a boyfriend and I didn't. *Wait a second, that guy* . . . That tall, dark haired guy in the crowd, the one not wearing a costume. He looked just like . . . *no*. No. Stop it. I had to stop this obsessing . . . but what if it was. Could it be him? Rob? He was supposed to be out of the country, running away from his troubled life, not haunting me in mine. I couldn't be sure from here, but it looked just like him: that perpetual self-satisfied grin, concealing the underlying dark mystery that begged to be solved.

I felt like I had just seen another ghost. It was too much for me to digest all at once. I started to get hot. Before I knew it, little beads of sweat began to trickle down my forehead and the faces in the crowd grew blurry as I listened to the remainder of my dad's speech. Then things got really blurry. The next thing I knew, I was beginning to lose my balance and I was tipping forward. Over the stage.

I have no recollection of actually falling off of the stage—just waking up in the arms of a man dressed in costume as a doctor, with an angst-filled Tones looking down at me. There was a crowd of curious onlookers that had formed a circle around me, taking in the spectacle before them. Snapping pictures with their camera phones and posting them to their social media networks, no doubt.

"Marley? Can you hear me? Are you okay?" the pretend doctor asked.

"I'm fine," I said, pausing to rub my lower back where I'd fallen. That would definitely leave a bruise. "I'm sorry. I must have just gotten overheated," I said to him. When his face began to come into focus a little better, he looked strangely familiar. Wait a minute . . . I knew that voice. *You have got to be kidding me.*

"Mr. Wright? I mean, ahh . . . Doctor. Doctor Wright?" I immediately corrected myself. I couldn't believe this was happening, *again*. Dr. John Wright, was the young, handsome resident who rounded on me, the two separate times that I was a patient at St. Aidan's hospital last month. It was never quite clear whether he was interested in me or if he was just inherently polite and charming. Seeing him right now felt way too strange. It's like he only existed to come to my rescue. Maybe fate *was* a real thing.

"I think you're going to be fine. You just fainted. When was the last time you ate?" Dr. Wright asked, purely professional.

"Oh, that's an excellent question. I don't really remember. Last night, maybe?"

"She's hypoglycemic . . ." I couldn't help but hear Tones shout to Dr. Wright and anyone else within earshot, as he pushed his way through the crowd. "If she doesn't eat often enough, she gets sick. Here, drink this." He shoved a Coke can in my face and I obeyed, allowing the sugar to work its way into my blood stream. I immediately felt better, as I wiped the wet drips from my face and pushed the can away. "I'm fine, Daddy." I looked up to see Dr. Wright's concerned expression.

“Still wearing those high heels, I see,” he said, with a kind smile that matched his kind eyes.

“I think I already told you, it would be asking too much of me to give up the heels.” I uttered a slight laugh and attempted to make light of the highly awkward situation that had started to unfold. “But, if I ever break something, I know who to call.” It felt like the gawking crowd encompassing us was eavesdropping in on our every word.

“Oh, that reminds me . . . Let me get you one of my business cards . . .” he said as an afterthought. He reached into the pocket of his grey jacket and produced a very professional looking card, complete with office, cell, and pager numbers. “Just in case you ever need anything. Day or night,” he added.

I looked up at him, slightly confused, unsure whether he had just asked me out or if he had merely extended a professional courtesy. Only time would tell.

CHAPTER 5

I woke early the next morning and took my usual four mile jog around the lake. The scenery of colorful trees made for a nice distraction from the burning in my lungs. Lake Genevieve is a 5,000 acre natural reservoir, owned by the city of Greenbriar. Every morning, rain or shine, I jogged at least three miles. This morning held the promise of turning into another beautiful fall day. I had mentally mapped out my upcoming article for the student paper as I ran. I had a few topics that I wanted to bring to the attention of the students, like free student services taken for granted, the rising costs of tuition, or, on a lighter note; the racy new uniforms the dance squad was forced to wear. However, I was under strict orders from Doc to write about Rose's attack on campus, warning other young female students to put their safety first. He wanted me to remind them to use the buddy system, not to walk alone at night on campus, to keep their dorm rooms locked, and to point out 'safe spots' on campus. I had also planned on stopping by St. Aidan's hospital, immediately after I finished my classes. I knew Rose didn't have much family here, so I really wanted to be there for her when she woke up.

After my run, I raced through the shower and dressed rather quickly. I decided to wear my thigh-high brown suede boots, short floral print dress, and tan furry vest—a little present I'd bought myself at Nordstrom's earlier that Fall. I had purchased it on my 'emergencies only' credit card; the bill went to my dad, so I would have to think of a clever excuse when the time came—a talent I had spent years cultivating. But after my brush with death, I felt I deserved it. I headed over to campus and endured a full day of three classes, back to back. Each class seemed to drag on and on. I was so consumed with my own personal matters that I couldn't focus on the subject matter at hand, especially in my worthless elective course, Intro to Environmental Studies. In order to fight off sleep, I subconsciously began filling up every available space in my sheet of notebook paper with notes on Rose's attack.

What did I know, exactly? I continued to scribble and draw inane items, like the white car with the detachable siren, fallen leaves, blood splatters—all objects in the clouded portrait of the unknown madman with a maniacal look in his eyes. I continued to draw and jot things down until a coherent thought or chain of thoughts came to mind, subconsciously, and scribbling them down. I had a very distinct feeling, deep down in the pit of my stomach, that this was the source of my fidgeting. I got the sense that there was something missing here. A rather obvious puzzle piece: the pink elephant in the room, but what?

After my last class, I walked over to the library to get some work done on my upcoming article. I decided to give Matty a call and ask him about any other brutal attacks on females in the area. It was time to start connecting the dots.

"Little sis . . . What can I do ya for?" As usual, Matty had answered his cell immediately, never wanting to miss what could potentially be an emergency call from the boss's daughter. Matty was not my biological older brother, but he may as well have been. He was my dad's best friend and loyal employee.

"Hey, big brother, what's cookin'? How's your love life?" I asked, attempting to make small talk about his latest girlfriend, Beth. I didn't want him to think the only reason for my phone call was because I needed a favor. It didn't take long for Matty to fill me in on the latest news about his love life, before he cut to the chase and asked me for the real purpose of my call.

"So . . . ?" The word carried a question mark at the end. "You generally only call me if you need something, so what is it?"

"Matty, what makes you think I need a favor? I was just checkin' in."

There was a long pause at the other end of the line. "Mmm hmm . . . not buying it. *Please*, don't ask me to do anything illegal today. Your Dad has me on a short leash these days."

"Nothing illegal, I don't think . . . I was just wondering, is there any chance you can somehow look in your nifty little police database for any instances where a woman was attacked? Well, not just attacked but brutally beaten . . . specifically. Or any other recent unsolved cases in the area, say, where a woman was missing or killed?"

"I think I already know where you're going with this one. This is about your friend, Rose, right?" he said, with a sigh. Before I could answer, he added, "I don't have to look in any nifty little database to tell you that a soccer mom, about forty-five minutes away over in Bellfield, was attacked last week; in the same fashion your friend was. The husband said she'd left the house for work early that morning and never returned home. Cops found her in her mini-van, pulled off to the side of the road, hazards on, just like Rose. She was beaten within an inch of her life. The only main difference was that this woman was a pretty, young soccer mom, not a co-ed."

"What? Are you saying that Rose isn't pretty?" I asked defensively.

"Seriously? What I'm saying is that Rose is a college student and the other victim is not. She was about ten years older than Rose. Geez . . . Take it easy."

"Sorry, I guess I'm just a little on edge."

"Okay . . ." Matty replied slowly, understandably apprehensive about continuing. "There's another woman. A graduate student over at Stratford U was reported missing about seven days ago." He added, "I know all of this from watching the news. Nothing illegal about getting this information. You should try it sometime," Matty said sarcastically and chuckled to himself.

“Are you serious?” I asked him incredulously, as I squeezed my cell tighter against my ear, worried I might miss something. “That’s three women in the past week.” I rubbed my temples, gripping them with the thumb and pinkie fingers of my left hand.

“Three? No, just two.”

“No, three. Rose is one, the soccer mom is two, and the missing grad student makes three.”

“If we’re going to assume that Rose was attacked by the same man who attacked these other women.”

“Of course I am assuming they were all attacked by the same person. Why shouldn’t I? It’s moronic not to.”

“Right, and jumping to swooping conclusions and making huge assumptions is not your style at all,” he said, in a condescending tone.

“Listen here, smart ass.” I gave it right back him, half kidding and half annoyed, shocked that he didn’t immediately agree with the connections I had just made. “It makes perfect sense. What did the other two women look like?”

“Ahh, let me just check here.”

“Where are you checking?”

“Google . . . Looks like they were fairly young, reasonably hot, Caucasian, petite, brunette.”

“It sounds like you just described Rose, to a T,” I said, before ending the call. That should give him something to think about.

I ended up finding a cozy nook in the school library where I could write in peace, without being bothered by any noise or other students. Before I even began to type the first word of my article about Rose's attack on campus, I knew I had to give it an edge. What would both help me to solve this case and make for a sexier story? I decided that a decent beginning would be to search the web for traits of serial killers. I wanted to find out exactly what made people do these horrific acts and why. So I gave myself a little crash course in criminal psychology over the next couple of hours. I figured that a smart way to catch this guy would first be to get inside his head. I needed to understand his thought process a little better. I wasn't a psych student, I was a journalist. *What did I know about this stuff?* I was suddenly feeling glad that I chose 'Abnormal Psychology' as my other elective class for Fall semester, which at least allowed me a modicum of knowledge on the topic.

After conducting several very basic internet searches for 'psychological disorders and serial killers,' the same term kept popping up among every credible site I came across: '*Anti-Social Personality Disorder.*' This was noted as the distinctive mental illness for someone capable of committing heinous crimes such as rape, murder, torture, etc. Individuals with this particular condition were often referred to as Psychopaths or Sociopaths. I learned that most were men, who did not experience fear or empathy. They had no scruples or reluctance to hurt others; they were quite capable of evil, malicious behavior. They were ruthless, yet also unselfconsciously personable. Because they lacked a fear response or empathy, they tended to be under-stimulated under ordinary circumstances, which was why they sought out thrills, including the thrill of rape, murder, and torture, or just breaking laws or rules. A lot of times, as children, this personality type would torture animals. They were convincing and continuous liars, always able to adjust their version of themselves and the truth to fit whatever the person or situation called for.

There was an abrupt slam of a door from somewhere nearby and it caused me to nearly leap out of my seat. I hadn't even realized quite how scary the subject matter at hand was until that point. I was on edge: this was some creepy shit.

I swung past Cat's office on my way out of the library, grateful to see that she had not left for the night but was still plugging away at her computer.

I peeked my head in the door. "Knock, knock. Got a quick question for ya."

"I take it you're finally ready to discuss what happened the other day?" she replied. Her eyes remained glued to her computer screen, yet she somehow she knew it was me. After all, she was psychic.

I paused and looked at her curiously. "Oh, sorry. You meant . . . with the whole ghost thing . . . No. No. Not really. I have an unrelated question though. Sociopaths, psychopaths, Anti-Social Personality Disorder. What can you tell me?"

Cat looked up at me from her computer screen with a sullen expression. Suddenly, I had her undivided attention. "Well, those are all very relative terms." She was clearly amused by my question. "What exactly would you like to know?"

"Just some basics. Distinguishing characteristics, that sort of thing."

"Well, people often like them. They can seem quite normal to those around them, who are frequently shocked to discover what horrible things they have done to others for personal pleasure, and personal gain . . . That is to say, typically sexual, often violent pleasure. Not all of them are horrible. Some are smarmy used car dealers or crooked politicians, but at the extreme, they can be sexual sadists who torture for pleasure. There's also a high genetic component, with some childhood sexual and or physical abuse sometimes playing a contributory role as well. If you hang around with them very long, you will eventually note that they tend to be cold, calculating, relatively fearless, sensation seeking, and yet smooth. Sociopaths look sane; in fact, they are very good at pretending to be sane and normal, except they are anything but." Cat's eyes never wavered from mine. She always made me feel like she was reading my mind.

"So, what about psychotic features? I mean, you're telling me that sociopaths are crazy, but they just sound like they have issues . .

. major personality flaws. Obviously, serious ones. But do they hear voices, or think they're their Santa Claus, or talk to themselves?"

Cat paused and mulled this last question over for a moment, before answering slowly with the ease and confidence of a professional psychologist who had schooled thousands on the ins and outs of the human mind for years. "A psychotic sociopath is not unheard of, but they are not very functional. They're usually in prison or institutionalized most of their life, constantly attacking guards and prisoners, and in isolation as a result. What's this about, if I may ask?"

"You may. I'm writing an article for the student paper. I just need to get some facts straight, that's all." I cleared my throat before continuing, hoping she wouldn't press me for further details. "So, in other words, they . . . ahh . . . I mean sociopaths, are more common than any one of us would realize?"

"More common and far more dangerous. Perhaps even more so than they realize." She lowered her rimless glasses down below the bridge of her nose and stared at me quite seriously. "You're talking about someone far worse than anything imaginable. You're talking about evil in human form . . . a living, breathing *Monster*."

CHAPTER 6

That night, I hopped into my convertible and drove across town to St. Aidan's Hospital. My mind was flooded with thoughts about my masked man. I was laboring under the assumption that he had to be sociopath, and according to my research, he was a textbook example of someone with Anti-Social Personality Disorder. It was just my luck that I stumbled across what was undeniably the worst personality type known to man: the type of person incapable of feeling any sort of emotion or empathy for anyone or anything. *Someone who couldn't feel.* The idea of it made my skin crawl, causing me to scratch a nonexistent itch on my arms at the thought of it.

I walked into the cold, sterile intensive care unit on the fourth floor. I found its eerie silence to be unsettling. I wasn't sure what to expect: just more commotion, I suppose—medical people draped in surgical gear, bursting through the corridors with a bloody patient on a stretcher, screaming words like '*stat.*' The woman at the reception desk informed me that Rose had been moved out of the intensive care unit and into her own room on the fifth floor. I wanted to shout for joy and jump up and down, this was the best news I've had all day. I sprinted right back to the elevator, conscious of the obnoxious click-clack sound my heels made as they slapped against the tile floor. I was so anxious to see my friend alive and alert, it hadn't even dawned on me to ask for directions, let alone her room number. I pushed the button marked '5' and waited impatiently for transport.

I wondered how long she had been awake and if anyone had alerted her parents. The only thing I knew about them was that they were divorced and lived somewhere in Kansas. The elevator doors opened at a snail's pace as I arrived on the fifth floor. The presence of the man waiting in the vestibule behind the elevator doors gave me a start, catching me unawares as the elevator doors opened with a loud 'ding.' There, in the vestibule, was a rather imposing presence of a tall dark stranger. Our eyes caught each other's for a quick moment. There was something odd about him, but I couldn't put my finger on it. He held his hand out against the cold steel of the elevator door, as a courtesy, to stop it from shutting on us. As I walked out, he walked in. For some reason, a peculiar feeling washed over me. Like the kind you get when you're not quite vomitus, but the feeling right before when you know something is off. Safely in the corridor on the fifth floor, I turned to glance over my shoulder at the man once more, as the elevator doors closed slowly in front him. He was still staring right at me as the doors closed and I could've sworn he had the slightest scowl on his face that inadvertently made me quiver.

I found myself wandering around the third floor, searching for a nurse or someone else official who could help me locate Rose's room. I finally came across a nurses' station, cheerfully decorated with cut-outs of smiling pumpkins and scarecrows. A ceramic jack-o'-lantern with a crooked mouth stared back at me from the countertop.

"Like I just told the gentleman who left, visiting hours are from 7AM to 7PM, unless you're immediate family." The chubby nurse's eyes never left her computer screen as she spoke. Her name tag indicated that her name was 'Becky R.'

"Well, I'm her sister . . . umm . . . Sonya."

Nurse Becky finally looked up from her computer screen, addressing me with a look of skepticism. "If you say so. Just across the hall." She pointed a chubby index finger with chipped violet nail varnish to a room located directly behind me; its door was wide open. "Room 522," she said, with her eyes narrowed eyes and a sardonic tilt to her head.

"Thanks for your help. I'm just going to go check in on my sister now."

I peeked my head into Rose's tiny hospital room. Judging from the empty stillness of the quiet room, I knew immediately that Rose was probably sleeping. On tippy-toes, I softly crossed the room and took the cornflower blue leather seat next to her bed. The dim room felt cold, unlived in, due to the lack of any warm sentiments such as flowers or cards. I immediately regretted not stopping to pick something up. *Tomorrow, I'll come back and bring something cheerful and bright. Yellow daisies, those would work. No . . . Sunflowers. Sunflowers would be perfect and maybe a silly card with one of those cute wrinkly dogs; wearing a funny hat . . . No . . . I got it—one of those cards that plays a funny song when you open them.* My mind flashed back to a birthday card that Jade had given me a few years back that played the sound of applause whenever you opened it up. No matter how many times I heard that applause, it brightened my day. I opened it so many times that the sound finally stopped working.

I took a deep breath and exhaled slowly through my mouth. My brain couldn't process the incomprehensible sight before me. Maybe I should have mentally prepared myself a little bit better before just barging in there. I didn't expect her to look quite like she did. My stomach heaved as I studied the patchwork of deep purple bruises covering her eyes, which faded into a brighter magenta rimmed with the putrid shade of a rotten chartreuse. Blue veins were visible beneath the thin, milky white of her flesh, giving the appearance of a roadmap etched onto her body. She must have been chilly with only the papery, lightweight hospital gown to cover her. I pulled the white sheet and blanket up to her chest. Next to the bed was a small dresser with two drawers. I opened the top drawer to find a phonebook, a bible, and a pen. The drawer beneath contained a folded white blanket, which I shook open and placed on top of her still, weak body. "There that should help," I said softly, and gently brushed some stray strands of mousy brown hair off her forehead and behind her ear. Her lips looked dry and cracked, so I reached into my bag for some lip balm and very softly rubbed it onto her lips, trying not to wake her as I did so.

I could feel the stinging prickles of tears begin to form behind my eyes. At first, I tried to fight them from coming. I wanted to stay strong for her, as if my steadfast composure would somehow make her feel better, should she wake up. But I didn't stand a chance against the sloppy, wet tears that poured from my eyes like rain showers. This was immediately followed by shallow breaths and ugly painful sobs that escaped from my heaving chest.

"I'm so sorry, Rose," I whispered to her in between sobs. "You don't deserve this. You're gonna be just fine. I'll help you make it through this." I reached for one of her limp, lifeless hands and enclosed it inside of my warm hands.

My mind wandered back to my Mother. What would she have done in a situation like this? What would she have said to comfort her? Certain members of my family still brag about my Mother's healing touch and her innate ability to always say just the right thing at the right moment. I think, in a situation like this, she probably would have just prayed. What else was left?

I closed my eyes, bowed my head, and recalled the words to the "Hail Mary' prayer that the nuns always made us recite in High School. 'Hail Mary, full of grace, the Lord is—ahh—with thee." *That was it: the Lord is with thee*. "Thy Kingdom come—"

I stopped abruptly when I felt the cold, child-like hand that I was holding begin to move. Suddenly, Rose's breathing seemed to become more labored, made more noticeable by the rise and fall of her chest. Her eyelashes fluttered as the lids of her eyes began to blink softly. She tried moving her mouth a little bit and gave her nose a little twitch. I noticed her toes wiggle under the blankets. I was about to scream out for a nurse, when I heard Rose mutter something. "Fff . . . . Eff."

"What? What was that, Rose? It's okay," I said softly, encouraging her to repeat herself before the nurses came running in.

"Ufff," Rose repeated herself again, "Uff." Her eyes opened briefly before quickly closing; her lips followed suit.

Shit! What was she trying to say? Eff? What was Eff? She was trying to communicate with me, most likely attempting to tell me the name of the person who did this to her. And I had absolutely no clue what she meant.

"You need to leave, now!" I heard Nurse Becky's voice yell at me as she came charging into the room, with another nurse trailing closely behind.

"She . . . she just woke up! She spoke. She, she, she tried to tell me something!" I stuttered as I announced frantically, with the grace of a football player wearing toe shoes and a tutu.

"We'll take it from here! You need to go! Doctor, her blood pressure's skyrocketing!" Becky's voice had risen to a shout. She screamed as she swiftly began to work on Rose, checking her pulse and studying some kind of graphs that a machine next to the bed had printed out.

A short, white-haired man, wearing a white lab coat and with a stethoscope around his neck, charged in, demanding to know what her vitals were.

On my way out of the room, I tripped over some sort of monitor because I wasn't paying attention to where I was going, unable to peel my eyes away from the scene before me. *Was she still awake? Did she slip back into her coma? What the hell just happened?*

CHAPTER 7

I woke up the next morning with thoughts of Rose weighing heavily on my mind. I forced myself to stop obsessing over things that were out of my control and jumped out of bed. I threw on my favorite sweatshirt with 'Greenbriar U' written across the chest, an old pair of black running shorts, and white Asics before I hit my usual tree-lined running trail that wrapped around Lake Genevieve. There was nothing like a little exercise to help me clear my thoughts and straighten out my head. I had so much on my mind and I still didn't feel one hundred percent, since my dramatic fainting spell two nights previously. I took off at a slower pace than usual until I found a steady rhythm. Just as my breathing became more labored, I noticed another jogger making his way toward me. As he slowly came into focus, I could see it was Ryan Duff, my neighbor-slash-plumber. I gave him a friendly wave, with no intention of stopping. I hated trying to speak when I was mid run, sweaty, and short of breath.

"Howdy, neighbor! How are those pipes treatin' ya?" Ryan Duff slowed down to jog in place.

It took me a minute to realize he was talking about my leaky faucet. "Oh, yeah, my pipes are just . . . great," I replied awkwardly, not sure of what to say next. “Thanks again . . . How’s everything with you?”

“Can’t complain,” he said, wiping the sweat from his mouth with his shoulder. His face was flushed red and his bald head glistened with sweat. He seemed to look different, outdoors in the sun’s bright light. I was able to get a clearer look at him. Muscular, tall, well-kempt: He appeared to be in excellent shape. “I heard about what happened to Rose . . . I mean, that girl on campus. She’s a friend of yours, isn’t she?” Ryan seemed rather intrigued by the situation and it struck me as odd that he knew Rose’s name *and* that she was a friend of mine.

“How did you know—?” I stopped myself. I didn’t want my neighbor to feel like I was interrogating him. Plus, this story was all over the news. “Yes . . . she is. She’s still unconscious. She was viciously attacked and left for dead. Only a complete psycho could have done that, someone without any sort of feeling.” I felt my blood begin to boil at the thought of it. I’d be lying if I didn’t admit that my stomach didn’t flip each time I thought of her. In fact . . . Rose was saying something last night resembling ‘Uff.’ Like Duff? My mind was beginning to wander. . . *Uff, like Ryan Duff?*

“I saw it on the news last night,” he said, with surprisingly flat affect, breaking my train of thought.

“She didn’t deserve this. No one does.” Unsure of how to wrap up this little conversation of ours, I looked down at my feet demurely as my mind wandered back to Rose.

“Well, I’m sure she’ll be just fine,” he replied dismissively, like it was just something that happens sometimes, like tornadoes or chicken pox.

“Well, that remains to be seen,” I replied, ever so slightly taken aback by his flippantness.

“I forgot to mention it the other day, but I have a big Halloween bash every year. I wanted to extend you an invite. It’s Saturday night: wear a costume, and bring a friend. Hell, bring ten friends if you want to.”

Of course, I had heard about the legendary parties thrown at Ryan Duff’s house. I believe most people likened him to Jay Gatsby, and his parties were compared to those out of a Fitzgerald novel—on a much smaller scale, of course. I knew that the town’s elite frequented his parties, sometimes even celebrities. I had often watched the spectacle from my dock, as the booming music and festivities were hard to ignore.

“Thanks, I’ll try to make it.” I briefly wondered if he threw these elaborate parties in the hopes that his long-lost love would walk through the door. I felt the need to romanticize everything. In reality, he was probably just a perv.

I returned home sweaty and out of breath. After chugging a glass of cold water, I indulged in a long steamy shower, scrubbing and exfoliating every inch with a lavender scented gel and loofah. I shampooed my hair twice, and applied a deep conditioner to rehydrate my ends. While the conditioner worked its magic, I shaved my legs and whitened my teeth, before rinsing off. I felt spectacularly clean as I slipped on my old peach robe and fuzzy grey bunny slippers that Jade had bought me as a congratulatory gift the previous month, for solving my first case. I flipped on the flat screen television mounted to bedroom my wall, as I combed through the dripping wet tangles in my long hair. I turned on the local news station, WKKP. I aimed the remote at the screen and cranked up the volume, so I could hear over the loud vibrations of the blow-dryer. The young male reporter was just beginning to discuss a breaking story out of central Illinois. '*A dangerous man with an extensive psychiatric history has escaped Long Bridge Psychiatric Institute for the criminally insane, in Springfield. Authorities warn that he is armed and highly dangerous.*' Just then, the screen flashed to an older photo of a young white man with a prominent scar on his left cheek, his lips poised in a smirk. His smiling eyes were an unusual shade of dark brown, more black than brown would be an accurate description: small and round, with a soul-less quality to them. His chestnut brown hair was somewhat long and wavy; it swept across his forehead, slightly obscuring one eye. You could tell he was crazy just by looking at him. '*Charles Skinner is a 27-year-old Caucasian male. He is considered to be very dangerous and possibly armed. Viewers are urged to contact the Springfield police department if they see anyone matching this description.*' The reporter spoke with a mildly troubled tone.

“Creep-store,” I said to my reflection and proceeded to get ready for another long day at school. I threw my hair up on top of my head in a loose bun. I applied an extra layer of moisturizer over my face and neck, as my skin felt particularly dry today. A quick coat of mascara, a layer of translucent shiny lip gloss, and a squirt of Chanel perfume. I longed for the styles of Bridget Bardot, Grace Kelly, and Sophia Loren to reappear. Eras when females dressed like ladies, and not strung out, heroine-addicted teenage boys. The styles that embraced the female sensuality and enhanced it, not hid it.

I was 5’6 and 118 pounds. Even reasonably tall and skinny, I could barely pull off the current style. Lucky for me, I wasn’t a complete slave to fashion; I just loved clothes and shopping. I pulled on some dark skinny jeans, a lightweight yellow sweater, and my light brown suede boots. I was good to go. I grabbed my usual banana and granola bar on my way out and headed to my morning classes.

Later that afternoon, I received a call from Doc Warner after my last class of the day, “She’s starting to wake up,” he said, without any sort of formal greeting.

“What? She’s awake?” I wanted to scream. I reined in my excitement, so I could hear the details.

"I didn't say she was awake, I said she's starting to wake up. Details, Marley. It's the little things that matter," Doc preached. "You know what you need to do."

"I'm on it." I needed to get to Rose and fast. The sooner I could learn any kind of information from her, the better chance we had at catching this monster before he hurt someone else or found Rose to finish what he'd started.

"And Marley . . . tread lightly."

"Don't I always?"

I made it over to St. Aidan's Hospital within forty minutes of Doc's call and managed to stop by a flower shop on the way. I entered Rose's room with a big bouquet of sunflowers and a greeting card. "How's our little patient doing?" I hollered cheerfully at the doorway.

The room was still silent and after I was able to see around the curtain, I saw that Rose was sleeping. I set the vase and card down on the bedside table so that the sunny flowers would be the first thing that she saw when she opened her eyes again. I gently tiptoed out of her room and back into the lively hallway on the other side of the door. I was surprised to see Nurse Becky from last night still on duty. She must have been helping another patient when I came in and that's why I hadn't noticed her before. I decided to stop at her desk on my way out. Much like last night, she worked hard at feigning busy-ness.

“I’m sorry to interrupt but could I just ask you a question?” I asked her timidly, a little afraid that she might reach across the counter and punch me. Instead, she stared at me blankly and spoke into the phone’s receiver.

“Can you hold on a second? I still want that cheesy potato recipe from you, girl,” she said to the other person on the line, as if it were life and death that she added yet one more cheesy casserole dish to her repertoire, contributing to the flabby roles of fat that padded her already enormous ass. “What is it?” She covered the receiver with her hand and shot me a nasty look of impatience.

“What did that guy look like?”

Nurse Becky looked at me, dumbfounded, signaling that she had no idea what *guy* I was referring to. “Excuse me? What guy are you talkin’ about?” she asked me, clearly irritated that she’d had to put her cheesy potato casserole recipe on hold for me.

“Oh, my bad. You remember: the man visiting Rose last night, right before I came in. He asked you if he could visit her and said that he was her brother.”

“Uh, let’s see,” she said, as she tapped her acrylic fingernails, attached to her chubby little finger-sausages; against her desk. “I don’t recall. I’m the only one here right now, so I’m a little preoccupied.”

I ignored her beastly attitude and continued to stare at her blankly, without backing down like she had hoped.

“I don’t know, tall, white, brunette. He seemed a little on the shy side.”

"You didn't happen to get his name, did you?" I asked Nurse Becky skeptically, already knowing the answer. I'm sure she was too busy, being the only nurse here last night and all.

"Nope. Like I said, I've been a little busy here."

"Alright, well, could I give you my name and number and maybe you could just call or text me if you remember anything?" I asked her, already knowing full well that she would toss it into the trash can as soon as I turned to leave. I thanked her again and headed down the cold hallway.

"Wait a minute!" Nurse Becky hollered after me down the hall. "I just remembered something. He had a scar. Her brother. He had a nasty scar across his cheek."

CHAPTER 8

That evening, after leaving the hospital, I was headed over to my Dad's house for family dinner. On the way, I picked up my cell and dialed Doc Warner's number. I filled him in on my encounter with Rose, but I also needed some advice.

"I need some professional advice. I have a hunch about something and I just need some direction, I guess you could say."

"And you already know what I'm going to say. A good reporter never ignores a hunch."

"That's exactly what I thought you would say." I cleared my throat before I continued to explain myself. "I don't know if you heard about Charles Skinner? He escaped from a hospital for the criminally insane down in Springfield."

"Ah, yes. I think I overheard something about that on NPR this morning. What about him?" I could tell I had Doc's attention. He sounded intrigued.

"Well . . . Don't you think it's an odd coincidence that three women were attacked or killed right after this psychopath escaped an insane asylum?"

"Well, you already know my answer to that question, too."

I mulled that over for a moment. "Ahh, yes, that's right. There is no such thing as a coincidence."

"You got it. See? You didn't even need to call. You answered your own questions with the exact answers I would have given."

"I guess that makes you the voice inside my head," I teased, and quickly applied a layer of lip balm on my lips. "In that case, I'm planning on driving down to Springfield, later on this week. Maybe Saturday. I'll need to talk with any family member that knew him, and the guards at the facility where he escaped."

Doc understood my plan. We both knew that by doing just that, I would be painting a more precise picture of my suspect, adding another brushstroke to the nebulous painting of Charles Skinner, with each person who knew him well.

I pulled up to my Dad's house. There was something so comforting, so nostalgic about returning to my childhood home. It always made me feel warm and fuzzy. The aroma of Italian cooking filled the kitchen and my stomach began to growl. I hadn't even realized I was hungry until then.

"Hello, Family! The boss is in the house," I hollered to anyone within listening range, as I hung up my coat in the already full entryway closet. The floor of the coat closet was still stacked wall to wall with old board games and toys from my childhood.

"In here!" Jade's voice bellowed from the kitchen.

I walked into the kitchen to find Granny Annie in the middle of some sort of how-to lesson in playing beer pong. Matty and Grandpa

Frank were not exactly a captive audience. Both sat around the table, arms folded across their chests, unsure of exactly what to make of the situation. Jade kept score, while Matty continued to try throwing the balls into the red plastic cups and Grandpa Frank just looked confused. Normally, a scene such as this would surprise most people, but for my family it was perfectly normal. My Granny Annie was always fun to be around: adventurous and full of surprises. "Marley, come join us! I'll show ya how to play. You'll love it," Grannie Annie said excitedly and motioned for me to come join them.

"Mom, I don't know where you pick this stuff up from!" my Dad said under his breath, with a roll of his eyes.

"Probably from one of her college boyfriends," I said teasingly.

"What's this? College boyfriends?" Granny Annie chuckled, playing along, the eternal good sport. "Who told?"

"Annie, I don't understand the purpose of this damn game. Why do I need to throw the ball into a beer before I can drink it?" Grandpa Frank asked rhetorically, while he rubbed his temples. The perpetual skeptic, he looked the part, with his wire rimmed glasses and prim and proper navy blue blazer with a white collared shirt underneath. Not a wrinkle was visible anywhere on his starched grey trousers; not a single grey hair was out of place on his head.

Before Annie could further elaborate on the rules of beer pong, a loud burst of hip-hop music began to emit from her nearby cell phone. I couldn't quite recognize it at first, but as I listened, I recognized the familiar Nicki Minaj tune. The song did not go unnoticed by Jade and me, as we exchanged knowing smiles, followed by silly, childish expressions. We were all too familiar with Granny Annie's entertaining shenanigans.

"I don't quite get that part either," Matty chimed in, agreeing with Grandpa Frank. Matty grabbed a beer, removed the Ping-Pong ball, tilted his glass slightly toward Grandpa Frank, and said, "Were too old for this game. Cheers."

"I'll toast to that. Cheers," Grandpa Frank replied, as he removed the ball from his glass as well.

"What ya cookin', Pops?" I decided to join my dad over at the stove, as I tied an apron around my waist.

"Tonight, we've got pasta with a spicy Arrabiata sauce, homemade spinach pasta—none of that boxed crap—garlic bread and Grandpa made his famous Italian wedding soup." He handed me a large wooden spoon that had seen better days. "Which could use a stir, if you don't mind," he said, motioning his head in the direction of the steaming pot of soup, dangerously close to boiling over. I quickly grabbed the spoon and gave the soup a slow, thorough stir. The miniature meatballs, fresh escarole, and chicken broth combined together to make the best soup I've ever had. Such a remembered taste from my childhood, the mere aroma of it sent me to a different time and place. I turned down the burner to a lower heat and peeked my head in the oven to check on the garlic bread.

"Tones, did you mean to burn your garlic bread?"

"Aw dammit, Freddy!" Tones hollered over his shoulder at Jade, discernibly blaming her for the burnt bread. "You're too busy with that stupid Ping-Pong game! You're too young to be playing that anyhow!" His feisty Italian temper was as normal an occurrence in our house as was Granny Annie's eccentricities and my high heels.

"Don't pop a vein, Tones. I'm just keeping score," Jade shouted right back to him, far too involved in the score-keeping than her task at hand.

"I got it," I said calmly and grabbed the tray out of the oven. "Everyone relax . . . its only bread." I tossed the burnt bread into the trash bin and returned to stirring the soup. I hovered my face over the hot, steamy pot of soup, closing my eyes and allowing the steam to open up my pores.

"Now, what the hell do you think you're doing? Get your face out of the damn soup," Tones said incredulously, with a shake of his head, before he muttered some choice Italian expletives under his breath.

"Did Matty tell you about the connection I made with Charles Skinner and the three women who were attacked?" I ignored his temperamental mood and looked him square in the eyes. "I mean, you have to admit, that's a pretty unusual coincidence. Just sayin'. . ."

Tones didn't say a word; instead, he merely shot me a look that said, *Stay out of it this time*. I had known him well enough to know the differences between his dead-serious looks and his looks that are . . . well . . . on-the-fence type looks. There was no mistaking his steely gaze this time around, definitely a dead-serious one. "I'm telling you: DO NOT play around with this case. I'm *not* confirming or denying anything—"

"Which basically means you're confirming that there might be a connection," I cut him off excitedly.

"Don't become a liability! I will not have you out there flaunting yourself as bait for every scumbag in the greater Chicago area!" His voice had risen again to a loud roar, as he firmly pointed his sauce covered spatula in my direction that sent little red splotches everywhere, onto the stove top and white marbled floor. The laughter and voices in the room fell silent. The only audible noise was the sizzling pot of Italian wedding soup.

Yes, it was confirmed. He was dead serious this time and I did not want to piss off Tones. Then again, what he didn't know wouldn't hurt him.

CHAPTER 9

I dropped by the public library the following day, to access some public records that I wouldn't be able to find at the library on campus; like old newspaper articles and deeds. It was Wednesday afternoon and the sun seemed to be setting earlier than normal, as the dismal skies took on a look of foreboding. The damp wind began to pick up, carrying a breath of rain on its lips. The public library was a five story brick building in downtown Greenbriar, sandwiched in between city hall and the Bureau of Tourism. It always had the odor of glue and mold. I found myself almost subconsciously shoving my hands in my pockets at the thought of the disgusting layer of vile germs that coated every book like dust. The first floor was dedicated to fiction for all age groups. The upper levels housed the historical documents, periodicals, anything nonfiction. I hiked up three flights of stairs to find a quiet space in a corner, where I could conduct my research with some modesty. The last thing I needed was someone to see me searching 'paranormal entities' on the computer. After all, I was a professional reporter now. I had a reputation to uphold. If word got out that I was 'ghost-hunting,' I could kiss my career as a serious journalist goodbye. Besides, I had zero experience with the supernatural, which I supposed was fortunate in a lot of ways. But, I was a writer. Curiosity was my nature. I was not capable of turning a blind eye to anything. If I learned of something unexplainable, I wouldn't be able to sleep until I had some basic understanding of it.

After searching through pages and pages of sketchy looking sites, along with sites boasting complete and utter nonsense, I narrowed my search down to sources that seemed to have a modicum of credibility. Those sites all had pretty much the same information on ghostly hauntings. According to a seemingly reputable ghost-hunting site, there are seven signs to look for if you sense your house may be haunted. 'In order to determine the validity of your haunting, you must do the following: listen for any voices or unusual sounds (such as banging, knocking, doors slamming, etc.), electrical appliances turning on or off, doors opening or shutting on their own, unexplainable human like shadows, feeling of being watched, objects moving on their own, and last, but certainly not least, cold spots.

I came across hundreds of sites where people were claiming to have had first-hand experiences with ghosts. One woman from Seattle insisted that she was awakened every night at three AM by something or someone pinning her down. She was petrified and pleaded for advice from anyone who was reading. *How awful.* I mean, seriously? I felt so sorry for her. Then, the left, more logical, side of my brain began to take over and I wondered if it was a hoax or just written by a schizophrenic homicidal maniac with nothing better to do. I continued to sort through more legitimate looking sites and I found a couple of sites boasting quotations from Dr. Lynn Hopkins: Criminal Psychologist and medium. I couldn't help but smile a little. I was proud not only to know her personally now, but to have her on my own little paranormal team.

Out of the corner of my eye, I noticed a man waltzing into my little section of the library. He was wearing a long black trench coat that matched the color of his unwashed hair and unshaven beard stubble. His skin was an ashen shade of white. He paused to look at me, almost curiously, before taking a seat directly across the table from me. He unfolded a wrinkled newspaper in front of him and occupied himself. *Really*? There was a ton of empty space in this library—five floors just filled with seats—and he couldn't find another place to park his creepy ass? Just my luck. I peered up from my computer screen.

Our eyes met and I gave him a little nod, as if to say, *'I see you; now don't bother me.'* although he probably took it as a look of seduction. Oh God, what if he was the '*Boogeyman'*? *Nah* . . . I reassured myself. *This guy clearly looks like a bum who just wanted to come out of the cold to warm up*. At least that's what I told myself. I cleared my throat and continued my research.

Ghosts, ghosts, ghosts...focus. Alright, I needed to find out two more things. First, I needed to look up how to get rid of the ghosts and then I needed to figure out why they are where they are to begin with. After I finished up my research, I would head up to the fourth floor to see if I could dig up old newspaper articles on microfilm and any other historical information I could find on the hotel and surrounding property.

"You're gonna die! The Boogeyman's coming to get you," he taunted me.

"What?" I asked him, outraged by his sudden outburst. "Get away from me!" I instantly grabbed my things as I jumped from my seat.

"You're a walking dead girl." His perverse laughter filled the small stale space between us. He began laughing harder now, almost uncontrollably. "Look at the pretty little dead girl!" he repeated, as he sang the words in a sing-song tone, while shaking his head back and forth, and baring his crooked teeth. He was so close, I could smell the reek of his sweat and body odor.

"Go to Hell," I snapped, before I ran out of the room. I began my nervous descent down the stairwell and nearly toppled over a little old man who was just standing there, staring at me in concern. He looked at me and adjusted his glasses. "What's the matter sweetie? You got the Boogeyman after ya?"

"You have no idea," I said to the old man before taking off. I looked back behind me. At the top of the stairs, I saw the maniac just standing there, laughing hysterically to himself.

Other gaping onlookers stood there observing the bizarre scene of events as they unfolded in front of them, but no one said anything. A girl scout troop stood at the base of the stairs with their troop leader, looking scared, and an elderly couple clung to each other tightly as if a bomb were about to go off. A man in a blue uniform with a flashlight and a can of mace strapped to his waist, presumably the on duty security guard, came running inside. A cloud of smoke followed him in; it was clear that he was outside on a smoke break, instead of doing his job. I merely rolled my eyes at him as I fled the library. I ran through the exit doors and back outside into the gloomy night air.

CHAPTER 10

On my way home, I stopped by the country market, my favorite little spot that boasted all local/organic products at reasonable prices. The small parking lot was filled with pumpkins of all sizes, various shades of mums, and towering bales of hay, all available for purchase outside. I pushed through the doors and grabbed a basket. The store was filled with the magical scents of apple pie and cinnamon rolls. I bypassed the small section of canned and pickled goods, making my way to the deli. I selected a whole chicken, deciding that maybe home-made chicken noodle soup would be a fun culinary challenge. I needed to distract myself by doing something with my hands: something to relieve my mind from all the dark thoughts of hauntings and Boogeymen. The subject matter at hand was beginning to get under my skin a little bit. Okay, a lot. No . . . that's still not accurate. I had to be honest with myself and I would be lying if I didn't admit that I was frightened.

The vegetables were located next to the deli. I carefully selected carrots, leeks, and celery for my soup. I noticed a big brown spot on the celery, so I set it back down to pick up another bag, when I heard a whisper, '*Marley.*' I turned on my heel, expecting to see a familiar stranger standing behind me, but there was no one. I took a moment to look around the little store, filled with shoppers. No one looked particularly familiar. *Hmm.* Maybe I just imagined it, or maybe Addy's ghost had followed me. Maybe there was another Marley in the store. *I'll stick with that theory for now,* I thought and took a deep breath. Suddenly, I was in a hurry to get behind the safe confines of my own walls and I sped the whole way home, as rain began to fall from the sky and sounds of thunder boomed in the air, like fireworks on the Fourth of July.

After I made it home, I was uneasy about being there alone. Frightened of my own shadow, I turned on every light in my house and cranked up the music as loud as it could go—something upbeat and soothing, like Louis Armstrong. I flipped on the television for some company, but it seemed like every channel was only airing horror movies. Night of the Living Dead, The Shining—normally, I would have been thrilled about the prospect of nothing to do but veg on the sofa under a heaping pile of blankets, with a bowl of popcorn and a marathon of horror flicks. But not tonight. Back in the kitchen, I worked quickly, chopping, stirring, and seasoning. As the lyrics to La Vie En Rose filled my home, I finally began to feel relaxed, as my hands worked in a steady, constant motion. My stomach began to rumble as the comforting scent of chicken noodle soup began to fill the kitchen of my quaint log cabin.

I turned to the refrigerator and reached for a carton of Orange Juice, took off the cap, and chugged it straight from the bottle. I glanced out the kitchen window to see the waves rippling in the lake and the ferocious wind causing tree branches and leaves to rustle. The rain seemed to be pouring from the sky in buckets, which made me happy to be inside safe and dry.

Just as I began to turn my eyes away, I caught a glimpse of a dark figure out of the corner of my eye. I dropped the carton on the floor and felt my socked feet grow cold from the wet juice puddle. I looked up at the square-shaped window above my sink. *Nothing.* I closed the blinds frantically, nearly ripping the cord from the frame as I did so. I grabbed a butcher knife from the drawer, before I ran to the glass French doors off the kitchen to make sure they were locked. That's when I saw the dark figure again, across the family room, at the opposite window. It was a man dressed in black and he was pressing his face against the glass, peering in. My heart nearly stopped as I leapt across the room for my cell phone, to dial the police. A loud moan escaped my lips as I slipped in the juice puddle and my body clumsily slammed onto the hard tiled floor.

The dark figure had already vanished from the window, but where did he go? Who was circling my house, peering in the windows? My fingers couldn't find the right keys on the phone; it was difficult to focus on the numbers with this panic raging through me. I tried to stop my hands from shaking but I couldn't.

"Shit!" I yelled, frustrated with myself. The soothing, melodic sounds of Louis's voice continued to fill the space all around me; the pot on the stove was now boiling and bubbling over. Then I heard a loud knock at the door. No, not a knock, but a pounding, door rattling knock. I ran to the door to get a good look at the culprit through the peep-hole, when I noticed Ryan Duff's bald head gleaming in the glow from the moonlight, leaning in close to the eye hole, looking back at me. My heart beat slowed just a little as the feeling of relief trickled over me.

I unlocked the door and opened it slowly, with a confused expression on my face. "Ryan? What are you doing?" I asked him, highly irritated, as I rubbed the palm of my left hand over my sore backside, which was throbbing in pain from my fall. "You scared the hell out of me."

"Well, your power seems to be working just fine! It's your hearing that I'm not so sure about," he exclaimed, trying to disguise his annoyance with comedy.

"What?" I yelled back, unable to hear him over the music. "Ah, hang on, Ryan. Let me turn that down." I left the door open, signaling it was alright for him to let himself in, as I jogged over to turn the volume down on the receiver.

"You really scared the hell out me!" I exclaimed, trying to mask the terrified expression from my face.

"I scared the hell out of you? I've been banging on the windows and the doors for the last five damn minutes. I saw your car parked out front, so I knew you were home. A transformer on our street was struck by lightning. Half the houses on this side of the lake are out of power. I just thought I'd check to see if yours was out."

I looked up at him, still confused, and didn't say a word. I had no idea how to respond to that and I was quickly beginning to feel foolish. He stood there, holding my gaze, handsome in his black North Face puffer vest, dark washed jeans, and sneakers.

"Look, with all the shit going on around here lately . . . well . . . I just thought I'd keep an eye out. That's all. Single girl . . . living alone out here in the middle of nowhere," Ryan continued, as his eyes carefully glanced around the room. He shoved his hands into the pockets of his jeans and finally brought his eyes up to meet mine.

I honestly couldn't decipher if he was hitting on me, if he was a creepy pervert, or if he was legitimately concerned about my wellbeing. Maybe all three. Or maybe I was off completely on all counts.

He took a deep breath. "Look, your Uncle Wayne's a close friend of mine. He's not here, but I am. Literally here—I live right next door. I just wanna make sure you're safe, at least until they catch this creep."

"I see . . . Well, that's admirable, I suppose . . . but I'm tougher than I look. Smarter too," I added flirtatiously. "Not to mention, my dad is the Sherriff, so I've pretty much got the county police at my beck and call." I did my best not to sound cocky, but still came off that way.

"I don't care if your Dad is the President of the United States. I know all about you, little girl," he said, serious now, his dark eyes piercing through the invisible shield of my steely exterior. "You go looking for trouble; it doesn't go lookin' for you. You're headstrong. You think you're invincible, but you're not. What are ya? About a buck ten?"

“Pardon? Buck . . . what?” I asked, with my nose scrunched into a funny expression, as I did my best to politely ignore his last remarks.

“You know, a buck ten. A hundred and ten pounds, or so?”

“Like I said, I’m stronger than I look.” I laughed under my breath. “I lift weights, I’m on the college swim team, I ran track in high-school . . . Oh, and I know how to fire a gun. AND, I know Aikido; my dad’s had me in those classes since I was in Pampers. Anybody messes with me in a dark alley and they’ll be sorry. You can quote me on that.”

Ryan gave a sort of amused laugh, “Well, excuse me, Chuck Norris. I didn’t realize I was dealing with a trained professional here.” His grin bespoke a look of subtle amusement and something else—intrigue, maybe. “Look, all I’m saying is that I’ve read your articles. I listen to gossip. I know you’re strong but you’re no match for the monster that’s out there. Preying on girls just . . . like . . . you,” he said, while gently poking me in the chest with his index finger. He smelled like aftershave and soap.

I couldn’t help but think his whole speech about looking after me was . . . well . . . pretty endearing, really. Most girls would probably be totally turned on by the whole thing, but I remained reserved, impervious to his attention.

“Clearly,” I said, “Wayne forgot to mention that I can hold my own. You have no idea who . . . you’re . . . dealing . . . with.” I poked him right back in the chest with my index finger, as I spoke those last few words. I had forgotten that my soup was boiling over and probably burning, so I walked away from Ryan over to the stove to turn down the flame from under the chicken noodle soup. I grabbed a handful of paper towels and began cleaning up the liquid that had spilled over.

"Something smells good," Ryan said, following my lead into the kitchen, as he plopped down onto a barstool on the opposite side of the island, making himself right at home. I took that as my cue to invite him to stay for dinner. What was the harm? I really didn't want to be alone and I wouldn't mind getting to know this mystery neighbor of mine a little better.

We talked over steaming bowls of soup. When Ryan didn't seem fully satisfied with just the soup, I made grilled cheese sandwiches with tomato slices and set out a bowl of pretzels.

"You know what sounds really good?" he asked rhetorically, wide eyes smiling, "Ice cream."

"Got some!" I said proudly, retrieving not one but two containers from the freezer. Mint chocolate chip and chocolate peanut butter cup. "Oh, yeah, baby." Suddenly, my spirits were lifted and it seemed the anxiety from earlier had disappeared into the crisp night air.

"Talk dirty to me," Ryan teased back. "You know what goes really well with ice cream? Cookies."

"Well, you are in luck, because my friend Fuchsia has a cookie obsession and left a box here." I retrieved a half-eaten box of Oreos that was only missing a few. While I was up, I grabbed a box of

Twizzlers and bag of peanut butter M&M's. "I figure if we're gonna go for it, we should really do it right," I said.

"Whoa, I like your style." He jumped up from the stool and opened the refrigerator door, "Yes! Root Beer. What girl has Root Beer?"

"Again, not me . . . Friends."

"Sure. That's what they all say," he said, as he began to open up my cabinets until he found the glasses. Without any explanation, he scooped up the ice cream with a spoon and dropped the scoops into the glasses, filling the remaining space with the Root Beer.

"Why not top it off with some floats?"

"My thoughts exactly." We clinked glasses and sipped our floats. As the night continued, we laughed and exchanged stories. He asked me if I ate like this all the time and I assured him it was only on special occasions, like when my neighbor was stalking me.

"Hey, if we hurry, we can probably make it to Pizza Hut before it closes. Throw back a couple Supremes, maybe some of those cinnamon stick things with the icing on top."

About an hour later, I was feeling like my old self again and I had most likely consumed an entire day's worth of calories in one sitting. Ryan said he had to get home, but didn't mention why or what he was up to the rest of the night. Actually, our entire conversation seemed to be about me: my family, my friends, school.

I even told him about Rob. I really hadn't learned anything about Ryan. He was, in fact, still a mystery to me.

As I watched, Ryan walked out the door and then stopped and looked over his shoulder at me, smiling. The rain had let up and the night sky was flooded with stars. Ryan opened his car door. *Weird, I thought he drove a truck.* But he was climbing into a white four door sedan, just like the one seen driving away from the scene of the crime on campus.

CHAPTER 11

That night, as I lay in bed, wrapped up in my yellow polka dot duvet, my mind was going a mile a minute. Why was Ryan driving the same car that fit the description of the Boogeyman's car? What happened to the black truck that I usually saw him driving? It was just a little too much coincidence for me. I decided to call Jade and put her on a three-way call with Fuchsia. I needed some voices of reason.

"Hold on, Doll. Let me just pause my show. I'm right in the middle of "Who Wore What When?"

I could picture Fuchsia sprawled out on her mauve velvet sofa, most likely wearing something silky with matching high-heeled slippers. I was also certain that all her makeup was still done perfectly, hair too.

"So what?" Fuchsia asked flippantly. "He's a rich white man; he's allowed to have more than one car."

"That's not really the point, Fuchsia," Jade interjected. "He's allowed to have as many different cars as he wants, but a white four-door sedan that matches the description of the car being driven by the mysterious madman. Hmmm." Jade let out a dramatic sigh, followed by a yawn. "Oh yeah, and he's a middle aged white man . . . same as our Boogeyman. My Humanities teacher always says something about coincidences . . . let's see, what was that? Something about how they don't exist."

"You mean that there are no such things as coincidences?' I corrected her.

"Yeah, that's it," Jade replied and I heard my dad's familiar tone in the background shout out, "Frankie, off the phone! It's late!"

"Oops . . . busted, gotta run." Jade hung up, leaving Fuchsia and me to discuss the matter further.

"Well, what does your gut tell you to do?" Fuchsia asked.

"That's just it. For the first time ever, I can't seem to trust my instincts. It's like I can't seem to form a solid opinion on who Ryan Duff is. One minute, I feel like he this sort of protective big-brother type of figure. He always seems to be looking out for me in a weird way, but the next minute, I'll change my mind entirely. He'll do or say something that completely throws me for a loop and I'm back to square one."

"Maybe everything that you've been through lately has caused you to doubt yourself, when it should really be just the opposite." Fuchsia spoke softly and slowly, suddenly reflective and insightful, as opposed to dramatic and giddy.

"How do you mean?"

"Well, let's see here, missy. You met and pretty much fell in love with Rob, whose life you saved, who then repaid you by skipping town, leaving you to pick up the pieces; without so much as a goodbye."

"Well, let's not forget the car," I interjected, still finding it necessary to defend Rob for some strange reason.

"Oh . . . you mean the consolation prize?" Fuchsia laughed to herself. "That's even worse. Oh, yes, and lest we forget, your investigation uncovered that his dad is the one responsible for your mama's death. Then there's my personal favorite part, you did bite off somebody's nose and nearly get burned to death in the process." Fuchsia took a deep breath before continuing, "Please, just tell me that you will not bite off any more body parts! Now, what did I tell you about that?"

"Why does everyone keep obsessing over the nose thing? I mean, seriously, look at the story as a whole and the nose thing is the only part that everyone likes to gossip about."

"At least they're gossipin', sweetie-pie."

"What do you mean?"

"Well, if they weren't gossipin', you wouldn't be relevant now, would you?"

"Thanks, Fuch."

"Don't ever doubt the fabulous Fuchsia Darling. She knows all. Now, I have an idea that just may work. Are you available tomorrow night, say around seven?"

"I guess so. Dare I ask the fabulous Miss Darling why?"

"Don't ask, just wear all black . . . Lots of cleavage."

I spent the next ten minutes or so listening to Fuchsia's absurd plan, which she swore was both '*brilliant and seamless.*' I was too tired to second guess it or lay out my objections, so before I knew it, I found myself agreeing to go along with her plan and break into the home of my number one suspect, Ryan Duff.

The following morning, I awoke to a call from Glen McGuire. His voice was frantic and hushed.

"Yes, Miss Parker. I was wondering what kind of progress you're making on the . . . eh...shall we say, *situation* at my hotel."

"You mean the ghosts?" I asked Glen bluntly, a little annoyed that he always referred to the hauntings in his hotel as '*the situation.*' "Have you tried an exterminator?" I joked, biding what little time I had.

"Like pest control?" Glen asked, confused.

"Umm, no Glen, I was kidding." I hurriedly brushed off the ambivalence that my joke had created and came clean. "I'm sorry I haven't been in touch the last few days. I guess I've been sort of consumed with another case."

I had been dreading this call, as I knew it would come. I had been subconsciously putting off my investigation of the Brass Lantern Inn, mostly because I was extraordinarily uncomfortable with the subject matter and because it was starting to give me the creeps. Not to mention, I had my plate full with the Boogeyman investigation, which was not only personal but swiftly becoming more dire by the day. I simply could not just delay my investigation and leave it into the hands of law enforcement. Who knew how long that could take and how many more women could get hurt or killed in the meantime? Especially not because of some ridiculous ghost story. I was not a magician; I couldn't just mysteriously talk to the ghosts and make them go away. However, I felt like if there was ever a time I needed to pull a rabbit out of a hat, now was that time. I couldn't leave Glen hanging. Aside from the fact that this was my first paid job, I had given Glen my word, and now I had to produce. Produce what exactly . . . I hadn't yet figured out.

"The Boogeyman case?" He interrupted me, a surprisingly assertive tone in his voice. He cleared his throat and before I could respond, he cut me off. "It's all everyone in town is talking about. The Boogeyman terrorizing Greenbriar, and during Halloween, no less. Well, it sounds like something out of a horror movie."

Clearly, Glen had found the 'Boogeyman' case to be as fascinating as everyone else in Greenbriar, although I was slightly taken aback by his eager curiosities. Choosing my words carefully, I answered honestly, "Yes, but I'm really not at liberty to discuss it. At any rate, I think I have some good news for you." My voice suddenly became perky as I tried to put a positive spin on my complete lack of answers to his 'situation.' "I've been conducting a little research on hauntings, and needless to say, there is quite a bit out there. For the most part, though, all paths lead to the same place."

"Pardon?"

"That is to say . . . umm . . . with the overabundance of information out there, all the credible sources I could find seem to agree on one thing, which is that you need to find out specifically what the ghost wants and help to grant that wish so the spirit can cross over—or you can simply just ask it to leave." I cleared my throat and continued to talk out of my ass. "Now, I've been in touch with a local group who specializes in this sort of thing; they're out of Chicago. They call themselves, 'The Skeleton Crew,' and I think they'll be able to help us.

"What exactly do they do?"

"Well, they are ghost hunters . . . actually."

"I've never heard of such a thing. It sounds like it could be some kind of a moneymaking scheme."

"Well . . . I suppose that's a risk you have to be willing to take. On the bright side, I've been researching their website and you wouldn't believe all of the . . . ehh . . . all the people they have helped. The investigations they've successfully been a part of and all of the pictures posted, capturing what appear to be real ghosts. Also, I went to high school with the lead guy, Weenie . . . oops . . . um, I mean Larry. Larry Watson . . . Great guy." I rolled my eyes at the thought of Goth-clad Weenie Watson and his crew of ghost hunting buffoons. *Wonderful, now I would have to crawl on my hands and knees and beg Weenie to help me solve this case.* "You wouldn't believe all of the fancy equipment they use to monitor heat, light, sound waves. I feel like this is the next logical step," I said and crossed my fingers that Glen would not see through my smoke screen.

Glen agreed and I promised that I would hire the ghost-hunters and bring them out as soon as they were available.

I took a deep breath, sat up in bed, and flipped open my laptop. I typed the words 'Skeleton Crew Chicago,' into the Google search box and the first link to pop up was, without a doubt, Weenie's site. I clicked on the link and a black page popped up, while white smoke billowed dramatically from the bottom of the screen. A familiar haunting tune began to play, as bullet point graphics slowly began to appear across the middle of the screen. I think it was the piano riff from the old movie, 'Halloween,' which just so happened to be one of my favorites. The first bullet point that flashed up stated, 'Each year, one in every ten homes reports signs of supernatural occurrences.' I felt a little chill, causing the skin on my arms to resemble goose flesh.

'Every time you feel a cold breeze or catch a glimpse of a fleeting dark shadow, YOU'RE NOT ALONE,' the second bullet point read, suddenly the face of a decrepit skeleton emerged slowly from the center of the screen, blurring everything else into the background, then abruptly expanding to fill the width of the screen. The face began to whisper something inane, which became louder and louder as the face grew larger, until it reached a loud shrill screech. I jumped involuntarily, nearly throwing my computer off the bed. The skeleton disappeared and little black bats fluttered across the screen as the home page appeared, with a menu on the left hand side and a full length picture of Weenie Watson on the right.

Staying true to form, he was pictured wearing black leather pants, complete with a black leather vest, crocodile patterned boots, and a black belt with a silver skull and cross bones on the buckle. His once pale, weak arms were now bulging with lean muscle and a colorful assortment of tattoos. He had the same black eye makeup and shoulder length black hair that he'd had when I ran into him at the festival. If I were going to be honest with myself, I would admit that this whole dark mysterious façade was a little bit of a turn on, appealing to my bad-girl side, but I quickly blocked that thought far, far, far from my mind. He was still Weenie, the guy that peed his pants in high school and wore bow ties with matching suspenders every day.

The menu contained several links: *who we are, photos, pricing,* and *contact us.* I clicked on the photos link and was suddenly impressed to see roughly fifty or so individual links, documenting various jobs with photos and descriptions. I randomly clicked on one entitled, 'Old School House Road.' There were about ten photos of a dark street in the country, lit modestly by a single street light. I wasn't quite sure that I noticed anything unusual until I saw the little white orbs in the corner. The next photo caused my heart to leap up into my throat. There was no mistaking a white shadowy figure crossing the street and staring blankly into the camera. *Whoa, that was seriously spooky.*

The next photo was perhaps even more disturbing, Weenie was standing in the center of the photo; casually talking with his hands to someone in the distance, and the same white figure from the previous photo was standing right next to him. Close enough to kiss him. The figure was most likely male, although it was difficult to make out any distinctive characteristics.

"Oh my gosh, oh my gosh, ohhh my gosh! No freaking way!" I yelled, and slammed my computer shut. I took another deep breath, as I attempted to calm my nerves. I had not been expecting that. "Wow . . . Okay, Marley, pull it together," I said out loud, as I drew in another deep breath and forced myself to slowly open the computer back up, as if two boney hands would pop out and start choking me. I clicked on the 'contact us' button and Weenie's personal information popped up, both phone and email address.

Without hesitating, I dialed his number. Weenie answered hastily after the first ring and agreed to meet me that day, at two o'clock, after my classes were over. Business must have been pretty bad, seeing that he was available the same day I called. I had to tell him to slow down when he told me he could meet me in thirty minutes. I had quite the interesting day ahead of me with the ghost-hunter meeting this afternoon followed by Fuchsia's cockamamie plan to break into the Huff mansion tonight. *What the hell was I about to get myself into now?*

<u>CHAPTER 12</u>

I pulled into the Brass Lantern Inn at quarter after two, running a little behind schedule as usual. I saw Weenie's crew unloading what was a surprising amount of heavy equipment from the back of a black van, covered bumper to bumper with graphics of skeletons, ghosts, and goblins of sorts. The logo on the sides of the van read, 'Call the Skeleton Crew—*when you think you're alone . . . you're not.'*

Tones pulled into the vacant spot next to me in his Madison County Sherriff's cruiser. I had invited him to come, mostly because I thought he would get a kick out of this stuff but also because I felt it was wise to have someone official on hand, just in case things got really weird.

"What the hell are you getting your old man into here, Eddie?' My dad spoke with his habitual frankness and a look of skepticism clearly painted all over his face.

"I asked myself the very same thing this morning, Pops. The truth is, I have no idea what to expect. Just . . . uh . . . be nice. Capiche?" I asked him, trying to speak a language that he would have no qualms understanding.

"I got it . . . be cool. I invented cool."

I rolled my eyes at him and shook my head, as we made our way inside. Weenie and I made the introductions. He had a team of three additional 'investigators': Randy, an overweight, middle-aged, balding man wearing a black t-shirt and jeans, with a spider web tattooed on his right temple and Zed, an even heavier man, also wearing a black t-shirt and jeans whose right eye was slightly crossed, pointing in the direction of his nose, which I found very difficult not to stare at. Weenie informed us that Randy and Zed were twin brothers: fraternal not identical. Lastly, there was a woman, maybe in her late twenties, whom I initially mistook for a teenage boy. Her name was 'Mo,' short for Maureen, I hoped. Her shaved head, thick black rimmed glasses, and black leather jacket completed her androgynous ensemble. I was suddenly feeling a bit silly wearing my mother's pearl necklace—given to her from her mother the day she graduated college—along with my hot pink cashmere sweater, short skirt, and high-heeled wedges. I cleared my throat and brushed my freshly shampooed hair off my shoulders somewhat nervously. "Well, uh . . . shall we get started?" I asked hopefully, praying that this would not take too long. I was as eager to wrap up this afternoon's little ghost hunting party as I was to wrap up this job.

After what felt like an eternity but what was really more like an hour, the ghost crew seemed to have finished with their elaborate setting up of equipment. *Who knew ghost hunting could be so much work?* I spent most of my time surveying the area with my Dad, with Glen hot on our heels, overly eager to answer any and every question about the hotel and its origins. I was entirely too nice to ask him to just go away and let me get a sense of things on my own, which was fine as I had become an expert at feigning politeness.

"So, can you explain to me what all of this stuff is?" I addressed Weenie and tried not to notice the way his tattooed biceps flexed as he adjusted some sort of tall black rod with a small camera attached to the top. He gave his head a little shake, gently knocking away the long, bluntly cut black hair out of his dark eyes.

"Well, this stuff . . . as you put it, is thousands of dollars of top-notch ghost-hunting equipment." He shot me a coy smile that revealed mostly straight white teeth. "If there's anything here, we'll either hear it or see it. Chances are even greater that we'll hear something after we leave, rather than live."

I scrunched up my forehead, completely confused. "How do you mean . . . we'll have a better chance of *hearing* something later?"

"See this guy here?" Weenie pointed to a little black recording box, propped up on a table next to us. "This is an EVP box."

I looked at him again, with even more confusion. "What is an EVP box?"

"EVP stands for electronic voice phenomenon."

"Oh yeah, I think I read about that somewhere. That whole white noise, telekinesis thing."

"Telekinesis, huh? Someone's been doing her homework." Weenie seemed excited that I was speaking his morbid language.

“Easily impressed, I see,” I retorted, developing a jocular rapport with a man who was becoming harder and harder to imagine as the kid famous for peeing his pants, usually the brunt of everyone’s joke, the victim of harsh yet quite hilarious locker room pranks, and the recipient of disastrous food fights in the school cafeteria.

“It records communication from *the other side*.” He raised his eyebrows dramatically up and down, for effect. “No, seriously, you will be shocked at sounds this thing picks up. Words, noises, sometimes entire sentences, all from non-human sources. Last year we were over at an abandoned old barn in Wichita. Randy was bitten by something. I mean bitten hard. That night, we listened to the footage from the EVP and right after you hear Randy howl in pain, you hear this totally malevolent sounding voice that demanded us to leave.” Weenie had the habit of talking with his hands, making animated gestures for emphasis. For some reason, I couldn’t stop staring at his black fingernail polish and black leather bracelets. I pictured him sleeping in a red satin lined coffin, surrounded by black roses.

“Hmm . . . Really? You have the voice documented? On tape?” I tried to appear like a serious, unconvinced journalist and not the highly suggestible dip that most people mistook me for . . . Even if some of the time that were true. “And . . . this thingy?” I picked up another mysterious looking black box and fiddled with the buttons, then spoke into it, “Red-Rum, Red-Rum . . .” I used my best ‘Danny’ voice, from the ‘The Shining.’

Weenie didn't look amused; he just stared at me blankly.

"Sorry . . . couldn't resist," I explained, feeling extremely immature.

"Haven't changed since High School, I see," Weenie said, smiling.

"Why? What fun would that be?" I asked rhetorically.

"That's actually an EMF recording device. It picks up electronic fields over different frequencies."

"Layman's terms, please." I looked at him questioningly.

"Well, disruptions in electronic fields could mean ghosts."

"Aha."

"The rest is pretty straightforward: I mean, we've got flash lights, motion detectors, headset communicators, film, and extra batteries, of course."

"Oh, yeah." I scratched my head briefly. "Is it true that supernatural phenomena drain batteries quickly?"

Weenie looked amused as he replied, slightly flirtatiously, "Yeah, well, something like that."

"Let's get this party started!" Tones's voice hollered from down the hall. He looked bored, his hands stuffed into the pant pockets of his Sherriff's uniform.

I heard an annoying cackle coming from Glen, who seemed to be kissing up to my dad all morning. He laughed incessantly at all of Tones's jokes as he followed him around like a puppy dog, asking inane questions about day to day happenings at the Sherriff's station. If there was one thing Tones couldn't stand, it was when people didn't know when to stop talking or when to leave. Glen seemed to be holding steady at irritating both of those annoyances.

"Alright, let's do this!" Mo shouted, making muscles for effect, before grabbing the video camera in one hand, as she shoved a handful of batteries into the other.

Tones and I followed the crew slowly through each dimly lit room. Even with the lights on, it was still dark. The morning light slipped through slight cracks in the curtains, casting tall shadows onto the walls. Once again, I had the same creepy sensation as before. My heart was beating so fast from fear that something might jump out at me and the image would be so horrifying it would be forever implanted into my brain, never allowing me to sleep again. However, I charged forward, all the way through the second and third floors.

"Dammit, I'm out of batteries. Again!" Randy shouted incredulously, as if angry at the ghosts for sucking the life from his batteries. *How dare they*?

"Heads up!" Weenie shouted and tossed Randy two more batteries. "Man, its crazy how much energy there is in this place. It's just shredding right through our batteries," Weenie explained.

"So, have you seen any ghosts yet? This place haunted or what?" Tones asked with his usual impatience for anything that he doesn't whole-heartedly agree with.

"Well, Sherriff . . . it's not quite that black and white." Weenie hit the 'pause' button on his video camera and walked over to us, he spoke in a sort of deep, sultry whisper. "It's not like chasing the bad guys. The ghosts are very finicky and they feed off of the energy around them."

Tones rolled his eyes and resisted the urge to laugh out loud. "What *exactly* do you mean by *finicky*?" He wasn't buying this Venti-sized cup of bull shit.

"You can't just demand the ghosts to come out and have a discussion with you. Everything is on their terms; it all rides on their particular mood. There is no question that this place is teeming with all sorts of energies that . . . To be honest, even I can't begin to explain or understand, for that matter. Just . . . just bear with us. We're almost finished," Weenie said patiently with arms crossed over his chest and the perpetual fling of his long hair from his eyes.

Tones took an exasperated breath, "If you say so, Weenie," he replied, as he responded to a text message on his phone.

I sharply shoved my dad's side with my elbow. "Dad! Nobody's called him Weenie since High School. His name is Larry."

"Oh, but I thought you said his name was . . ." Tones voice trailed off as I poked my elbow into his side once again, signaling him to zip it. He instantly caught on. "Oh, I'm sorry. Larry," Tones said with a plastered smile, looking completely disconcerted. "Sorry, son. My apologies. I think the last time I saw you, you were a freshman in High School."

"No worries; it's cool, Sherriff. It looks like we just have a few more rooms left and then maybe an attic or something," Weenie explained, calmly and coolly, as if he was used to explaining the delicate temperaments of the paranormal to lay people just like us, time and time again. He had everything under control, or at least he played the part well.

About an hour later, we were back where we started, in the lobby of the hotel, sans the ghosts.

Weenie suggested that we all have a seat somewhere and look through the photos and various footage they had taken with their cameras, as well as their EVP audio tapes, because there was a good chance we missed something that was right in front of us the whole time. Then Glen suggested that we just get a table inside of the Pirates' Cove restaurant, on the first floor of the hotel. He then added that he wanted to 'bend Tones ear' about some issues he was having concerning zoning and panhandling, but not necessarily in that order.

All seven of us were seated at a large oblong table in front of the window that overlooked a lovely pond with a quaint, dilapidated wooden dock. Two mallards floated gracefully among the green moss and fallen leaves. We wasted no time getting down to business. Glen had some complimentary appetizers sent over, as he managed to Bogart my dad's time discussing his zoning issues. Weenie took a seat next to me, so I had a view of the photos up close and personal. I watched how the well-crafted muscles in his forearms seemed to jump a little each time he flipped to the next photo. If only he didn't wear those stupid black sweatbands around his wrists . . . I could probably be attracted to someone like . . . wait a minute . . . I could fill an entire page of *'if only'* when it came to Weenie Watson. *Concentrate*!

"Whoa . . . Did you see that?" Weenie nearly leapt from his seat. "Hold on, I'll go back." He quickly flipped back through the past several pictures, while Mo, Zed, and Randy jumped behind us to get a load of whatever Weenie was about to show us.

At first, it just looked like a nebulous sort of cloud next to a window, but as I looked closer, I could see it was actually a picture of a mirror that was reflecting the cloudy image standing next to the window. I could make out features of a woman's face. She was quite pretty and she appeared to be pointing to something toward the window. My eyeballs felt like they grew as wide as half dollars and I must have gone pale, because the next thing I knew, my Dad had jumped from his seat to rush to my side.

"What are we looking at here, kids?" Tones removed his reading glasses from his pocket, held them up to his eyes, and leaned in for a closer look. Everyone grew quiet—so quiet, I swore I could hear my own heartbeat. It was as if everyone was too afraid to break the tangible silence, like it might make the ghost in the picture disappear. Why was I holding my breath?

"What the . . . Hell?" my dad exclaimed.

I took a deep breath and began to laugh as I heard tones break the group silence. "That's a Ghost," I said proudly.

"There's your ghost, Miss Marley," Weenie said smugly, the only member of the group not even a little surprised about the cloudy figure on the screen before us. "A full blown apparition. Beautiful." Weenie seemed enamored with the image before him. "Mo, I want this up on the site, like five minutes ago." Mo was already typing fastidiously on her laptop, transmitting the picture for the whole world to view.

"Addy. Her name is Addy. We've met before," I said, smiling back at Weenie, equally smug. I could hear my dad over my shoulder drawing a deep breath, as if he simply could not take any more of this today.

Weenie shot me a morbidly flirtatious glance, as if the subject matter at hand was somehow a turn on for him. "What do you mean? Addy?" He was becoming overly excited as he tilted his body closer to mine. Suddenly, I was the center of his attentions.

"She whispered something in my ear, the only other time that I was here. I had sort of . . . put it out of my mind. It kinda freaked me out, to say the least."

"Do you mean to tell me that we have a 'Reciprocal Apparition' on our hands?" Weenie stared at me in disbelief, and then Zed reached across the table to give him a high five.

Both Tones and I looked at Weenie in utter confusion, unsure of what exactly was happening.

"Oh, sorry. A reciprocal apparition is totally rare." Weenie paused for dramatic effect and swept the shaggy chin length black hair behind his ears. I was once again distracted by all of the silver rings on his fingers and his black nail polish. *Was that a Rolex watch? I guess the ghost hunting biz was lucrative after all.* "It's a type of spirit phenomenon when both the ghost and the human can communicate." Weenie then nodded to Mo, signaling her to include this finding on their website alongside Addy's picture.

"Oh, come on. We weren't communicating, per se. *She* spoke; *I did not* speak back." I darted Mo a sharp glare and warned, "Mo, don't you even *think* about putting my name on that story."

Mo returned my glare with an even sharper, meaner stare.

"I'm sorry, *pretty please* don't include my name." I did not need Mo on my bad side. I was willing to bet she could bench press three of me. My eyes shifted back to the camera lens and safely away from Mo. "Wait a minute . . . is she pointing at something? The ghost, I mean," I asked anyone and everyone within ear shot.

"It looks like she's pointing out the window," Zed, the quiet obese one with the crossed eye chimed in. It was the first time I had heard him speak all day.

Mo held her masculine finger with the chewed up cuticle to the camera screen, addressing the way in which Addy had her finger pointed. "Look, she's definitely pointing out the window, all right. Glen, what room is this?" she demanded, in a military fashion.

Glen appeared to be too scared to get out of his seat and look at the picture. Reluctantly, he made his way around the table, and after a mere glance, informed us that it was the honeymoon suite on the third floor. He could tell by the striped wallpaper and scalloped drapes framing the window.

"We just recently renovated that suite, this last summer." Glen's voice cracked like a twelve year old boy's. He stood, fidgeting nervously, adjusting his glasses and crossing and uncrossing his arms.

"That could be the problem, right there," Weenie said. Sometimes renovating or changing something familiar will cause the spirits to become . . . angry and they might all of a sudden decide to make themselves known."

"Well, I think the most important question here is: *What* exactly is she pointing at?" I piped in, urging along the business at hand.

"Let's see here, that's the northeast corner of the building, which faces the pond." Glen cleared his throat, after his voice cracked yet again. "So, you're looking at it . . ." He pointed meekly through the window, to the pond in front of us.

"Hold on. Why don't we take a listen to the EVP recordings before we do anything else?" Weenie suggested. He was now a man who insisted on being in charge, after years of abuse from his more mature classmates. He wasn't fast enough to make the soccer team, he wasn't tall enough for basketball, or strong enough for football, IQ not high enough for honor roll, but he would be the authority on ghost hunting. I guess somebody had to do it. He retrieved the EVP machine, fast-forwarding it to the end of the tape.

"I figure, this is one of the very last rooms that we reached. So, if she did try to communicate with us, it would probably be at the end of the tape." He stopped the tape and I heard what sounded like loud static. We listened for a while longer and when our food arrived, Weenie let the EVP tape continue to play, so we could listen as we ate. The appetizers that Glen had sent over contained a wide array of fried food: onion rings, cheese sticks, hush puppies, and shrimp. There was also a plate of chocolate chip cookies. *Life in the*

Midwest, I thought, as I stared at the trays of diabetes and heart disease sitting in front me.

We all watched as Randy and Zed dove in first, wasting no time diving in and sampling each fried item, one tray after the next. Randy took a bite of a cheese stick and a streak of grease dribbled down his chin. I handed him a napkin.

I couldn't eat; my stomach was uneasy from the smell of grease as my mind reeled from the picture of Addy. Weenie, Tones, and I seemed to be the only people still listening to the white noise. There was a sudden mumbling of words spoken in a soft voice. Weenie pushed a button, stopped the tape, and rewound it back a little. The three of us exchanged wide-eyed glances and I sat up a little taller in my seat, bracing myself for what we were about to hear. Weenie played it again and turned up the volume louder.

I heard a voice of what could only be Addy. It was difficult to understand at first, so we listened to it at least ten times more. "*Can,*" was the only word we were able to clearly understand. We listened again. There was a clear *C* sound that began the first word, followed by second clear 'Ba' sound . . . ' At first it sounded like, *Can..bee* or *Cat-breeze*. Weenie made a few more adjustments to his fancy machine and we listened again.

"*Can't be,*" I shouted out.

"Maybe," Weenie said. "It's this second word I'm having trouble understanding. Let me just make one more adjustment here." He turned another knob and played the nebulous sound yet again.

My heart raced a little more with each playback. The first word was definitely *can't*. This time it sounded like *Can't-bre*.

"CAN'T BREATHE!" I yelled and jumped out of my seat, which caused the other patrons to stare curiously over at our table, like we weren't weird enough already. "CAN'T BREATHE! That's it. Get it? She's pointing out the window, down to the pond, and telling us that she can't breathe because she's trapped *under water*!" My voice made a funny, whiny sound at the end of my sentence. I couldn't sit still. *What did this mean? What was the next course of action?*

Weenie looked over at me in a way that was difficult to discern between annoyance and excitement.

I looked up at my dad and I could tell he was thinking the same thing I was. Tones made a fist and held it under his chin, a pensive look he only made when he was deep in thought; heavily analyzing the options laid out before him. He looked over at Glen, "Well, Glen, how do feel about draining that pond?"

CHAPTER 13

After we left the Brass Lantern Inn, I was far too excited to study for my upcoming test on controversial topics in Journalism, so I begged my Dad to let me head back to the Sherriff's station with him. We needed to discuss this situation further. I didn't want to drop the ball on this; I wanted to keep pushing through: solve this ghostly mystery, put the case to bed, and move on. The maintenance crew at the Inn was already in the process of draining the pond while we talked shop. It was a small pond; roughly around seven feet deep, so it wouldn't be long before we had a definitive answer. Tones agreed that I should stick around for a bit longer until the draining process was completed. He instructed Matty, his Deputy Sherriff, to go keep watch over things. Matty was under strict instructions to report back to Tones, often and immediately, with any findings.

Over a tin of homemade pizzelle cookies, lovingly made by one of my Dad's many adoring lady friends; we were mid debate over whether George Harrison or John Lennon had the more talent.

"Can I get you anything to drink?" Marilee interrupted, with her sweet old lady voice. She had to have been in her late seventies and she always smelled like mothballs. She had been my dad's secretary since he started as Sherriff. The lenses on her glasses were so thick, it amazed me that she could even see at all. Her clothing was always shades of pastels: floral blouses with matching cardigans that she had knitted herself. She knitted both Jade and me Christmas sweaters every year, which usually ended up in the Goodwill box. This year, my sweater had the word '*naughty*' knitted across the front, while Jade's said '*nice*.' Marilee's choice of attire today was no different: she wore a ruffled pink blouse with a pink sweater draped across her shoulders, complete with three strands of pearls and a sensible grey skirt. She wore a pair of gold rimmed glasses and another pair dangled around her neck.

"Just a couple of bottled waters would be great. Thank you," Tones shouted from behind his desk.

Marilee stopped and cupped her wrinkled, veiny hand to her ear. She was hard of hearing as well as legally blind.

"WATER!" He enunciated the word slowly, followed by a patient smile.

"Ok, sweetie, uh-huh," she replied and as she turned to leave, I noticed that her skirt was tucked into the back of her pantyhose, exposing her entire backside, which of course, displayed her enormous white granny panties.

My Dad and I looked at each other and giggled. "Dad, you've got to tell her."

"I'll have one of the girls in the office tell her. It's not my place," he said with his hands dismissively, making a funny face.

His cell phone rang. "Matty, whatcha got for me? Uh-huh. Yep...*Say what*?" My dad slowly set down his pizzelle cookie on a napkin. He had a cagey sort of look in his eyes. "Tell them not to touch a damn thing. I'll call Jack over at the Coroner's office myself. I'll be there in ten minutes." He shoved his phone back into his pants pocket and reached for his jacket from the back of his leather chair. "Well, kiddo. Once again, it looks like you're one hell of a detective. A bag of bones was just found at the bottom of the pond in front of the Brass Lantern Inn."

"No way! Oh my . . . gosh! This is so exciting! Can I go with you?" I asked eagerly, already knowing the answer.

"NO! I'll call you when I know more. Don't you have classes today?" he asked facetiously. When it came to my academics, my Dad never actually worried because I always kept my grades up, regardless of surrounding circumstances. Not to mention, I almost always made the Dean's list every semester.

"Mind if I stay here and work on a paper?" I asked, with seemingly innocent intentions.

He paused before answering, knowing full well that I would snoop the second the office door closed behind him. "Don't get into any trouble. You got it?" He shot me a frazzled glance before he slammed the door shut behind him.

"You better hurry!" I yelled after him. I removed a pen and notepad from my purse and made some incoherent notes that resembled chicken scratch. Okay, what did I know for sure? I began writing facts that I knew to be true: the hotel is clearly haunted, this started happening after the renovations began, and we have a young female ghost probably in her twenties—who was probably died by drowning. My research had shown that if ghosts tried to communicate, it was usually because they wanted or needed something. Addy had made it quite clear that she wanted us to check the pond. I wouldn't know for sure until the Coroner's office took a look.

Hmmm . . . I drummed my fingers on the desktop. I needed to access the computers in the Department of Records. However, this wasn't possible because I was not a county employee. Without my Dad or Matty next to me, I had zero authority. I mulled this over a moment or two longer, then picked up the office phone sitting upright on the desk in front of me. I hadn't used a land line in so long, I'd almost forgot how. I examined the list of extensions for the various departments located in the County building, which was taped onto the base of the phone. My eyes quickly scanned each extension on the list until I came to the Department of Records. I punched in the digits and waited for an answer. *Easy-Peasy.*

"Department of Records, this is Shane" His voice sounded as though he was around my age.

"Hi, Honey, this is Marilee up in the Sherriff's office." I used my best old lady voice, which was a combination of obnoxious and whiney, with a touch of the sniffles. "My arthritis is acting up today and I need a favor." I held my breath and waited to see if Shane bought my act.

"Of course, Ma'am. What can I help you with?"

"Well, Sherriff Tony wants me to cross check the name Addy, Addison, Adelaide, or anything close with any deaths in the last . . .

ten to twenty years or so." My voice waivered and I kept making an annoying sniffling sound, like I was trying to clear my runny nose. "I know it's a lot to ask, but you would really be doing this tired old lady a big favor."

"Well, I'm not sure I have the authority to do that, Ma'am. My supervisor isn't in the office right now. He stepped out to use the restroom. Maybe I should wait until he gets back."

"Oh, no. I don't think the Sherriff can wait any longer. He says he needs the information posthaste and we all know what a temper he's got on him." I gave a pitiful sounding laugh, followed by a little cough at the end.

"Yes, Ma'am." He gave a little chuckle in response, commiserating with me. "I wouldn't want to make the Sherriff mad. It might take a while though, ten years of files and all." Shane sounded skeptical about the whole situation.

"I'll tell you what. What's your boss's name, dear?"

"Steve."

"Alright, well, I'll talk to Steve and tell him that I insisted you check those files for me. I'll make sure that you don't get into any trouble." I sniffled again for good measure. I began to panic ever so slightly: if Supervisor Steve had just *stepped out*, that meant he probably was in the restroom, so he would be back in minutes, even seconds. Crosschecking the files sounded like it could take a lot longer. *How was I going to pull this off? I'd come up with something.*

"Yes Ma'am. Should I call you back after I check the files?"

"NO!" I said, practically screaming into the receiver in my normal sounding voice. "Ha, I mean, no thank you dear. I'll call you back in a little while." I hung up the phone, grabbed my purse, and raced down to the first level. The corridor that housed the restrooms, elevator banks, and soda machines was vacant. I stood against a concrete wall and pretended to check my cell phone, as I waited for Steve to exit the bathroom. Hopefully, I hadn't missed him. No one was coming in or out of the restroom doors, male or female. I took a deep breath and felt my heart rate increase, when I heard this disgusting farting sound coming from the men's room. *STEVE*! *Ehhh . . . Sick* . . . I exhaled slightly.

Lucky for me, it sounded like Supervisor Steve had a case of the runs. I couldn't help but make a disgusted face, mimicking vomiting motions when I heard the toilet flush, followed by running water from the sink and a loud vibration from the hand drying machine. *At least he practices good hygiene*, I thought to myself. I heard footsteps coming near the door. I had to think fast! So I dropped on my knees to the floor.

"Can I help you, miss?" A middle-aged balding man stood towering over me, presumably Supervisor Steve. He wore a plaid shirt and khaki pants.

"Oh, could you please?" I smiled up at him from the floor and squinted my left eye. "I'm looking for my contact. I was getting a drink at the water fountain and it fell out. I'm completely blind without it."

“Sure, did you check over here?” Steve pointed to a patch of floor by the fountain.

“Not very well,” I gave him my best helpless puppy dog look.

“I’ll start over there then,” he said kindly, and didn’t ask me any other questions, like who are you or why are you in this dank corner, searching for your contacts.

A few moments passed, maybe five at the most, before Steve spoke up again. “Well, I don’t think we’ll find your contact. Especially not on this white floor. You could search all day and probably not find it.”

“You know what, you’re right. It’s silly. I have more at home. Thank you for your help, though.” I flashed Supervisor Steve my brightest smile, as flirtatiously as humanly possible. “You are such a gentleman.” I reached out and touched his forearm.

Steve uttered a shy laugh; the poor guy had no idea what just hit him. His plump cheeks turned a bright shade of crimson. “Anytime. I’m here every day.” He gave me a little wave and turned to walk away.

“Wait! Umm, do you know where I can find the umm . . . uh . . . the person . . . who validates parking tickets?” Any idiot knew that person would most likely be close to the entrance of the building at a reception desk, but I was desperate for just a few extra minutes while Shane finished his search through their computer files.

“Well, that’s on the first floor. Right next to the front entrance; can’t miss it. Tell ‘em Steve sent ya.” He was nervous and he stuttered his words a little as he spoke. He turned to leave again.

"One more thing, do you have the time? I lost my watch and my phone is in the car." I threw my hands up in the air absentmindedly.

He glanced at his wristwatch, "Sure, it's quarter after."

"Almost quitting time," I teased with him again, pointing my finger at him and making a dumb ass little clicking sound. "Is that a Rolex?" I pointed to his cheap wristwatch with the chipped gold veneer band.

"Ha ha . . . That's a good one. I got it from Sears last year . . . Black Friday special, I think."

"Oh, you've got to be kidding me. It looks just like a real Rolex. You must have amazing taste."

"Thank you," Steve stammered, and his cheeks grew an even deeper shade of red. "Alrighty then, I've really got to go." Steve turned on his heel and gave me another timid little wave as he walked away. All I could do was hope that was all the time that Shane needed to finish his task. I ran back up the stairwell and back into my dad's office. I picked up the phone and dialed the extension for the records department, one more time.

"Department of Records, this is Shane."

"Shane dear, it's me, Marilee."

"Hi, Ma'am, I just finished checking our database and I couldn't find any female deaths corresponding with the name Addy or Adison, in Madison County, in the last ten years. It didn't take as long as I thought it would. Adison is an unusual name.'

"Huh. Well, are you sure? I mean, nothing stood out?" I tried to disguise the disappointment in my old lady voice.

“Yes Ma’am, I’m sure,” Shane replied, with his impeccable manners. “Can I make a suggestion?

“Sure, Dear.”

“You may want to check with missing persons.”

“Okay, thanks, Shane. I’ll do that.” Without thinking or really caring, I spoke the words in my normal voice before hanging up the phone. “Okay, so maybe I was wrong . . . but if I was wrong, then *who in the hell was in the pond? It never occurred to me to check with missing persons,* I said, talking to myself as Marilee walked back into the office. Apparently, she had misheard our simple water order because she sat two cans of Orange Crush on the desk, with a bowl of chips and salsa. As she turned to leave, I quickly reached over and yanked her skirt out of her pantyhose. She didn’t seem to notice, didn’t even react in any way.

At any rate, I probably needed Matty’s help at his point. I knew he was still over at the Brass Lantern Inn, helping with the skeletal remains found in the pond, but I also knew he would always make time for me, regardless of where he was or what he was doing. I dialed his cell.

“Little busy right now,” Matty answered the phone impatiently.

“I know, I’m sorry but I need your help. I can’t tell you exactly what it’s for but it’s important.”

“Right now? I’ve got a corpse on my hands.”

“Oh, slow down . . . my dad is there. Let him handle it and I don’t really think that a bag of bones is the same thing as a corpse.

Or is it?" I asked reflectively, unsure of the answer to my own question.

"Alright, smart ass. What can I do you for?"

"I need you to ask Kyle, your friend in the FBI if there was ever a missing persons report filed for a woman name Addy or Adison or Adelaide, or anything in the like; within the last ten to twenty years. Only in the town of Greenbriar, of course."

"No problem. I'll do it tomorrow morning when I'm back at the office."

"Matty, I really need you to do it now. I wouldn't ask you unless it was truly important."

"In the grand scheme of things, will it really matter if I find out now or twelve hours from now?"

"Actually, yes. It could make all the difference in world. Plus, if you don't . . . I'll tell Tones that you didn't really have the flu on Monday but you stayed home and played video games all day . . ."

"Oh, alright. For God's sake. Give me five minutes to call over there and I'll see what I can do."

"You're the best." I set my phone down on the cherry wood desk and admired the framed photos in front of me. My high school graduation picture sat in the corner next to Jade's cheerleading photo. Sandwiched in between the two of us was an old black and white photo of my mom, Faith. She was sitting in a field of daisies; her long legs were tanned and her blond hair fell at her waist. I was beginning to feel a little sentimental when my phone began to ring. The caller ID read '*BRO.*'

“Matty, geez . . . you work fast. What’s the word?”

“You’re lucky. Kyle happened to be at his desk when I called.”

“Why would you be surprised? Isn’t he just a paper pusher? I’m mean, he’s not like actually an agent, right?” I asked condescendingly, which Matty ignored.

He sighed before continuing. “Listen, there was a missing persons report filled out for an ‘Addy’ back in 2008.”

“I knew it. What’s the full name?”

“Hold on; let me check my notes.” I heard some commotion. he cleared his throat before he continued. “Here it is. Do you have a pen and paper handy? You’ll want to write this down because I’m not calling him again.”

“Got it. Shoot.”

“Date reported missing was May 18, 2008. Full name is Addison ‘Addy’ Jane Whitmore. She was thirty-three years old and was reported missing the day after her wedding.”

CHAPTER 14

I emptied a box of Cheerios into a bowl and topped it off with skim milk for dinner. I still couldn't believe what a day this was turning out to be. What I really wanted to do was stay inside my cozy house, safe from the howling wind, and the ghosts, not to mention the local predators. Clearly, that was not in the cards tonight. Ever since I had gotten back home, all I could do was obsess over my ghost. *Addison Jane Whitmore*. Who was she and what had happened to her? At least now I had a name that more than likely went with the bag of bones found in the pond today. I would do some detective work on the internet tomorrow and see what a simple Google search could pull up on her. This would also make an excellent piece for my upcoming article for the student newspaper.

About an hour later, I found myself hunched down into a ball next to Ryan Duff's garage. I was dressed in all black, camouflaging myself into the dark night sky. I even wore a black stocking cap, low over my ears. I watched as Fuchsia made her way up Ryan's long driveway. Her fishnet stockings, short skirt, and platforms were no match for the crisp fall night. She pressed the doorbell and waited impatiently, as she fiddled with her oversized hoop earrings and then removed a compact and powder puff from her handbag. She began to powder her nose and smack her lips together, ensuring that her coral lipstick was in the lines.

"PSSST . . . Stop fidgeting!!" I whispered loudly to her; she was beginning to make *me* anxious.

"I CAN'T HELP IT!" she whispered back, mouthing the words dramatically, with eyes wide underneath raised eyebrows.

I couldn't help but laugh, she was so awkward, and it was hilarious. Then I heard the door jerk open and a man's voice suspiciously asked, "Can I help you?"

Then I heard another man's voice respond in a deep growl, "Yes . . . oops . . . ha-ha . . . I mean yes." Fuchsia corrected her tone and repeated the word '*yes*' in a loud falsetto, followed by another inappropriate giggle.

Instinctively, I threw my hands over my agape mouth, to silence my laughter, which was nearly uncontrollable at this point. I forgot that Fuchsia had a hard time using her faux female voice when she got nervous, causing her natural, deep voice to come out.

"My car broke down, over there, in front of your house, and I was just wondering . . . if you might be able to help me. I left my cell phone at home, so I'm just stranded out here," Fuchsia said, before uttering another high pitched laugh.

"Oh, okay, sure... Let me just grab a flashlight and I'll take a look. I know a little bit about cars." And just like that, Ryan took the bait. He disappeared back inside his house for a moment, and then reappeared with a coat and a flashlight.

“Oh, I can’t thank you enough,” Fuchsia said again. “You are such a gentleman.” She spoke the word ‘*gentleman*’ in a high pitched tone. “I’m Fuchsia, by the way. Fuchsia Darling, but my friends call me Fee-fee.”

“Fee-fee?” Ryan’s replied, not so much to ensure that he heard the name correctly but to ask if Fee-fee was really her name.

I waited until Ryan was close enough to Fuchsia’s car and had his back turned toward me, before running up to the front door. He had left the front door unlocked, as I had predicted he would; making it easy for me to slip right in. I was laboring under the assumption that he would be alone. After all, I knew he was a bachelor, with no children. What I didn’t plan on was the tall blonde I saw standing approximately seven feet ahead of me, in the kitchen. She had her back to me, so I couldn’t get a good look at her face. She wore an apron over her short, tight, red dress, her black stiletto heels only making her already tall shape that much taller, thinner, and more severe. She pulled her long bleached blond hair over one shoulder and began humming to herself as she read over what appeared to be a recipe in a cookbook. I wasn’t sure what exactly she was cooking but I could smell the remnants of something burning in the oven and I heard something that sounded like water boiling over, making sharp hissing sounds as it dripped onto the hot burner. She didn’t seem to notice me as I quietly crept up the stairs to the second floor, leaving her blissfully unaware downstairs in the kitchen. I could be fast. Fuchsia and I had timed this whole scenario out, allowing me exactly four minutes inside the house. I stayed close to the wall as I continued to creep down the long hallway. I wasn't sure why, that's just how I'd always seen it done in cop shows. I entered the first room I came to, which looked like a guest suite. I gave it a quick glance; nothing that appeared to be of interest—just a double bed and a dresser. The room across the hall was nearly identical, unlived in. I continued on to the next room, which I presumed was the master bedroom, with a California king bed, covered with a satin duvet in deep shades of azure, gold and forest green. A large black frame sat on one of the mission style nightstands; showcasing a photo of Ryan with his arm around a beautiful blond woman. It was a logical assumption that the blonde in the photo was the same blonde burning dinner downstairs. I tip-toed carefully into the room and gently opened up the drawers in his dresser, one by one. The only thing I saw were perfectly folded clothes, color coordinated by drawer. Even his underwear was folded into neat little rows. I peeked under the bed: a large hunting rifle lay in an open case, with open boxes of ammo on top. *Interesting,* I thought to myself. My eyes frantically searched the room high and low, wall to wall. *Nothing.*

There was one last room at the end of the hall and I simply could not leave until I checked it out. The door was closed and the knob didn't budge as I tried opening it. Taking a deep breath, I removed a bobby-pin from the pocket of my jacket. I made sure to stash one for this very occasion, along with a pocket sized-neon pink-flashlight and my favorite go-to utensil, my military issue pocket knife. A gift from Tones, I always had it handy, especially since it had saved my life last month. I pried the pin open with my fingers, forming it gently into one long piece. I shoved the pin into the key hole, held my breath, and wiggled the pin. The knob turned easily and I saw exactly what I was looking for: *the lion's den.*

Ryan's office was by far the most attentively decorated room that I had seen in the entire house. It was obvious that he spent the majority of his time here. He must have just been up here because I could still smell a wisp of his cologne in the air. His aura was all around me, blanketing my senses.

My stomach gave a little lurch; a byproduct of the adrenaline and nerves. I felt acutely aware of my surroundings. My fingers felt cold and my mouth was dry as I studied the massive desk before me. It was like none I had ever seen. It was made of a heavy slab of stained wood that rested on top of sleek chrome legs. There were heads of deer and buffalo mounted to his walls, along with the largest bass I had ever seen, which hung above his desk. One thing was for sure: this guy loved to kill things.

I padded over to the gigantic desk and swiftly began opening drawers, fingering through their contents. I turned on my handy little flashlight and held it in between my teeth so I could use my hands to search. Every file, every pencil, every piece of paper was kept in immaculate order. Any item out of line would not be accepted; it was spotless. I flipped through his files, nothing. I was quickly losing hope and I couldn't shake the feeling of eyes on me. Like the feeling someone was looking at me.

My eyes raked the room, taking inventory of my surroundings. Where was this feeling coming from? There was no one hiding in the shadows, no obvious security cameras. There was, however, a large ornately decorated beautiful gold frame sitting on his desktop. Inside the frame was a black and white photo of a stunningly beautiful woman, wearing a delicate wispy white veil and a long sleeved white wedding gown, adorned with lace and beads. Judging by the more modern stylings of her hairstyle, makeup, veil and gown, I would guess that that it was taken somewhat recently. The woman's eyes had a haunting quality to them, giving me the feeling that she watched me as I shuffled through Ryan's things. I wondered briefly just who she was and why she gave me the creeps.

Just as I was about to give up, I opened the wide center drawer of the desk. Nothing there either: just a desk calendar, with events written down in perfect capitalized letters, a perfectly straight row of black pens, and a small square container that held silver paperclips. I noticed something just barely peeking from the corner of the desk calendar, so I lifted the edge of it upward, only to reveal dozens of photos. I immediately recognized a photo of myself standing on my balcony, drinking coffee and peering down at the boats on the lake. Then another photo was taken of me walking through the commons area on campus, wearing a jean jacket over my red striped sun-dress and talking animatedly with my hands to Doc, who was walking next me. We looked deeply engrossed in our conversation. A folded up newspaper article was taped to the back of that picture. I quickly unfolded it, careful not to rip it. It was my article from the school paper that I wrote last month on the death of Dean Cummings. I lifted up the calendar higher, only to find a sea of pictures hiding underneath. *Wait a minute . . . they are all of me.*

The flashlight was beginning to weigh too heavily on my teeth, so I set it down on the desk; aiming the light downward on the pictures. Each picture carefully plotted, every shot taken from a well scouted, camouflaged location. All were taken with the innate acuity of someone with a natural instinct for spying. And all of them had been taken completely unbeknownst to me.

I was not looking at the camera in any of the pictures; they were all action shots. I was either talking to someone else, swimming, or jogging. Anything I did in the public, he had documentation of, right here in this drawer. There was even a photo of Rob and me engrossed in a very passionate looking kiss, but I couldn't make out where it was taken. How long had he been stalking me? What was all of this about?

Before I could answer any looming questions, I checked my watch and I was three minutes over the allotted four minutes that I had to snoop. I had to get out of here, and fast. Surely, Ryan had realized by now that the battery in Fuchsia's car was merely unhooked, thereby eliminating the source of ignition to the engine. It's unreal what you can learn to do on the internet. The only major snag in our plan was how Fuchsia would explain the unhooked battery, but I was sure Fuchsia could think of something. She was good on her toes.

Suddenly, I heard the engine of a car start. I raced to the window to see Fuchsia's car was running and her head lights illuminating the dark road. My time was up. I walked out of the office and hastily made my way through the hallway on my tippy-toes and back down the steps. I paused and peeked my head around the corner, to see the blond woman still busy cooking and humming away.

I wasn't sure how to make it to the garage from there, but I had to find a way. This would probably be my only shot. I was here, I had to do it. My best guess was that the garage was off of the kitchen, as it usually is in most houses. My eyes frantically searched the kitchen and I spotted two doors. I thought it was safe to assume one of them led to the garage. I held my breath again, I leaned flat up against the wall in the dim hallway and watched the blond woman as she continued to sing, making her way around the kitchen. I waited until she bent down and opened the oven door. With her back to me, she was lifting a heavy roasting pan out of the oven. I used that as my opportunity to sneak across the kitchen and into what was hopefully the garage. When I was outside of Ryan's garage earlier, I had noticed a door that I could easily exit through. Right now . . .

Just as the blonde pulled out a black roast of sorts from the oven, I crept behind her and opened the first door I came to. It was definitely not the garage but a utility room. My heart started beating faster. What if I was wrong and neither door led to a garage? I held as still as a statue and listened to the blonde begin to shout expletives at her crispy black creation as she set it up on the counter and threw her oven mitts at it viciously. I reached for the knob on the other door, opened it, and before even looking to see what it was, I stepped in and closed the door behind me.

Luckily, I had chosen the correct door. I found myself in the cleanest garage I had even set foot in. The air carried the scent of bleach and fertilizer. The garage housed three cars, one motorcycle, two bicycles, and one four-wheeler. The white four-door sedan in question was nowhere to be found. There was a black truck, a white Porsche, and the third car was covered with a brown tarp. Just I was about to lift up the tarp, I heard a door slam from inside the house and garbled voices. Ryan was back and he was in the very next room, talking to the blonde. I had to hurry.

I swiftly threw up the heavy cloth tarp over the trunk, only to reveal the white sedan. I hurriedly reached into the pocket of my black jeans for my little flashlight and couldn't find it. *Hmm . . . I wonder where I left that thing.* Instead, I grabbed my cell out of my jacket pocket and found the flashlight app, which allowed me to use my phone as a flashlight. I shone the light on the plates. They were Illinois plates, not Indiana, like the Boogeyman's plates supposedly were; according to spike-through-the-nose Margie Reynolds. Maybe she was wrong. My stomach heaved again as I quickly switched my phone to camera mode and took a couple fast pictures of the plates, just in case. It wasn't like I would ever have the chance again. Maybe I would have Matty run them for me.

I was invigorated. I'd gotten exactly what I'd come for and uncovered even more. I shoved my cell back into my pocket and made my way to the door that would lead me outside. I gave my surrounding one final look over and walked through the doorway, into the cold night air and straight into Ryan Duff's broad muscular chest.

CHAPTER 15

"Ryan . . . HI!" I said stupidly, from behind wide eyes with dilated pupils, as the pale pallor of pure shock washed over my face, only magnifying my guilt. Ryan didn't respond; he just stood there with his arms crossed, waiting for an explanation.

"Oh, uh . . . I know this probably looks really strange but . . . uhh . . . the damndest thing happened." I gave a ditzy little laugh and before I could elaborate, Ryan cut me off.

"You wouldn't happen to know anything about a broken down Volkswagen? Would you?" he asked, his tone denoted the slightest hint of sarcasm.

"Ha... That's a good one. No. No. I would *not* know anything about that." I attempted to laugh yet again, but instead it came off like a strange dry cough. "No, I was looking for my . . . cat, actually. Her name is a . . . Puss-Puss. Pussy. Pussycat. Just like the song," I said awkwardly, in a sing-song tone, without a clue where I was going with my story of pussy the cat. "I have all kinds of pet names for her. Sometimes I just call her *cat*.'

"Pussy the cat, huh? That's a very creative name." It was clear that he was toying with me now, enjoying watching me squirm and ramble on about a non-existent cat. He looked one part amused and the other part irritated. "I didn't know ya had a cat." His eyes studied me narrowly, as he looked right through my story that was as transparent as cheap lingerie. The man was *STALKING* me! Of course he would already know if I did or did not have a cat. *God, I'm an idiot.*

"Yes. Well, it's not really my cat. It's my grandmother's cat. She's out of town for a few days, so I'm just cat-sitting. Actually. You haven't seen her around have you? Big, fluffy white thing." I couldn't seem to stop myself from rambling. I was busted and I was making up rambling stories about cat-sitting for my grandma's cat. I had to shut up. I ran out of words and just looked up at him. Ready to run or attack, whichever the situation called for.

"Funniest thing just happened," he said, completely ignoring my last inquiry into the whereabouts of my missing cat. "I was just flashed by a cross dresser who pretended to have a broken down car. Are you sure you wouldn't know anything about that?" He pressed me as he leaned in closer.

I reflexively shivered. *What do I say? What should I do next?* I felt like I had been trapped inside of a spider's web, awaiting my fate. I thought about what my Dad would advise me to do. *Deny, deny, deny. That's exactly what I'll do. He has absolutely no proof that I did anything illegal.* Then I heard a shrill ring coming from my pocket; it was my cell. *Saved by the bell.*

I retrieved my phone from my pocket, looked up at Ryan, and said, "Sorry. I've got to take this. It's my . . . um . . . grandmother. Probably checking on her cat."

“Oh, right. You better get that.” He shoved his hands into the pocket of his jeans and watched me intently as I began to walk off. I was gripping my keys in my hand and I decided to head straight for my car, so I could get away from him fast.

“Wait . . .”

Ryan’s voice may as well have been lightning striking my heels. I stopped dead in my tracks and turned slowly even though my gut told me to *run like hell.*

“You forgot this,” Ryan said. In the palm of his outstretched hand lay my neon pink flashlight.

An hour later, I was sitting in front of Fuchsia’s stone fireplace drinking lavender tea that she had made for me in a futile attempt at calming my nerves. I didn’t feel safe sleeping in my house tonight and decided that I would feel safer staying at Fuchsia’s place instead. I could have always gone home to my Dad’s house, but how could I possibly explain that to him? It would ultimately mean clueing him into my investigation and I could not possibly do that. He had enough on his plate: campaigning for re-election, the Boogeyman case, and Matty told me that my Dad’s blood pressure had been running high lately. The last thing I wanted to do was to add even more stress to his life.

But there was always Matty: he had access to confidential records, highly confidential, in fact. He could look up the license plates on the white sedan I found in Ryan’s garage. I would stop by the Sherriff's office first thing in the morning and bribe him with donuts. Once I figured out who that car was registered to, it would give me a new lead to follow, at the very least. Fuchsia walked into the small room, wearing a pink satin robe and matching turban. She was holding a tray with cookies and a pot of tea. "Fuchsia has some yummy snacks for you!" She spoke in her usual melodic sing-song tone, which always made me want to laugh, though I didn't dare.

"Thanks, Fuch. Maybe some more tea? My nerves are too rattled to eat anything."

"Oh, honey, look at you just withering away to nothing. When was the last time you ate anything?" Fuchsia had all the concern and care of a mother hen watching over her baby chicks. Before I could defend my newly thinner physique, she said, "I'm serious doll. You have got to put some meat back on those bones. Honestly, you look like a little ragamuffin. And your ends, when was the last time you had a trim? Highlights?" She lifted up my ends between her bejeweled fingers with blatant disgust. "Are those sweatpants?" She gasped, horrified at the sight of my old sweats, apparent dead-ends, and bony façade. "Oh, you know how I feel about SWEATPANTS!" Fuchsia began to make obnoxious pretend convulsions, as she rolled her eyes into the back of her head and made funny mock gagging sounds.

"Listen here, you caddy little vixen . . . I've been kind of consumed lately. I mean, between homework, my article, swim team, and now my new side job as an investigative journalist, I mean there just hasn't been any time left." I exhaled dramatically and I could feel the ball of stress begin to bunch up in my stomach like a tightly wound ball of knots. I needed a little break, just a few hours to forget about serial killers, ghosts, and perverts. I needed a distraction. I needed to go somewhere to clear my mind, relax, and rejuvenate . . . *Somewhere I could really find myself* . . . .

"Let's go to the mall," I said to Fuchsia, as I set my lukewarm mug of tea down on the coffee table and threw the afghan back onto the loveseat.

"Now, that's the spirit," Fuchsia said.

Greenbriar's mall was made up of two levels and six major department stores, with about two hundred smaller retail stores connecting them. Fuchsia insisted the first order of business was the salon inside of Nordstrom's, where her best friend Sebastian was patiently awaiting our arrival. I followed Sebastian back to the shampoo bowl where he busied himself adjusting the water temperature and selecting the right shampoo for my hair type. All the while, Fuchsia was insisting to him that I needed 'the works' and that he would have his work cut out for him.

Sebastian was nodding his head in agreement as he rolled up the sleeves on his white designer button down shirt and got to work, hastily scrubbing and sudsing my long locks with his fingertips. His coiffed blond hair and evenly fake spray tanned skin gave him the appearance of a Ken doll. He always made me feel like I was in a hurry, moving twice as fast as everyone else. He had a very Zen-like quality about him that put me at ease in his company. Also, because I found listening to him and Fuchsia banter back and forth about utter nonsensical topics, such as who had the bigger ass, was more entertaining than stand-up comedy. Two hours later, I was shampooed, trimmed, highlighted, blow-dried, and styled. While Sebastian took care of my hair, his assistant Tricia took care of my unpainted fingernails, which were now crafted into a beautifully rounded shade of baby pink.

It was getting late and the mall was on the verge of closing at any moment. Fuchsia had ventured out into the contemporary section of Nordstrom's, carefully selecting three new outfits for me to try on. Insisting that all three would look 'positively fetching' on me, she offered to buy them with her employee discount, insisting that I could just pay her back later.

"Fuchsia, is there anything you wanna tell me?"

She looked over at me, confused, and set down the outfits she was admiring as she stood in front of the full length mirror, holding them against her body, envisioning herself wearing them. "Anything you feel the need to get off your chest . . . so to speak?"

"What do you mean . . . so to speak? Just what exactly are you alluding to, little Miss Marley*? I am a lady.*"

I gave her a no-nonsense stare and raised an eyebrow dramatically high in her direction.

"Well, what did you want me to do?' She took a dramatic look at her sparkly fingernails, "Honey, if all else fails . . . you simply must flash."

CHAPTER 16

I got up early the following morning, *not* because I was diligent about getting an early start on my day but because I simply could not sleep. At around 5 AM, I decided to get up, make coffee, and start on some work in my office. If I had time, I would try to squeeze in a run before my first class started at 9:00.

I headed into my office, which was a spare bedroom that contained my most prized possessions. Inside the quaint room was a chunky old oak wood desk with my laptop and printer, crates of clothes that were either out of season or out of style, rows and rows of my books, and my favorite photos and accomplishments were framed on the wall. The first thing I did was pull my long, wild hair out of my face and tie it on top of my head into a bun. Then I entered the name Adison Jane Whitmore into the internet and searched for any type of background I could find. Nothing was coming up. I even tried typing the nickname 'Addy', with the last name Whitmore. Then I entered her full name and Greenbriar, Illinois after it. No obituary, no Facebook page, no noteworthy accomplishments on the internet anyway, nothing. So who was she? I texted Matty's cell and asked if they uncovered anything further after we spoke yesterday.

He texted back, '*Coroner's office has an anthropologist looking at bones- will be a while b4 they know. Go back to bed!*'

'Thanks Bro,' I texted back.

I screwed around on the internet a little bit more and also did an internet search for 'Ryan Duff and RDP plumbing.' Not much came up, other than RDP's website and a couple of other yellow page links. Next, I finished up a research project for my Mass Media and Communications class. I threw on some running clothes, stretched out by my front door, and headed out into the chilly autumn morning.

The sun was just beginning to rise from the hard, cold earth. I watched as a flock of geese flew away into the sky. The events of last night were weighing heavily on my mind. I hadn't yet figured out how I would explain to Ryan why I was in his house and why my flashlight was on his desk. Part of me didn't even care, considering I had just uncovered his big secret; that he was a stalker and I was his target. If anyone should be embarrassed here, clearly it was him. He had a gorgeous blonde cooking dinner in his kitchen, a picture of another beautiful woman-in a wedding dress-framed on his desk, and oodles of pictures of me hidden in his desk drawer. I mean, really . . . what a perv. I continued to think about the whole scenario as I ran and before I knew it I was coming up on mile marker 5. Sweaty and out of breath, I stopped for a quick break. I wiped the sweat from my forehead with my arm, then placed my hands back on my hips for another minute as I caught my breath. The sun was shining bright on the lake this morning, the running trail was lined with tall maple trees, and the only sounds around me were from birds chirping and leaves rustling.

As I made my way back home, I stopped at the end of my driveway to pick up a copy of this morning's paper. The front page headline read, 'Human remains found near Brass Lantern Inn.' I unfolded the paper and began to read as I headed to the front door. *'A plastic garbage bag filled with human bones was found in a pond, yesterday afternoon outside of the Brass Lantern Inn. An anthropologist from the state medical examiner's office is inspecting the skeletal remains of the adult bones. According to Sherriff Tony Parker, 'Investigators have gathered information from the remains and the Illinois Bureau of Investigation is entering that information into the FBI's missing person's database. Both local authorities and the FBI will continue to investigate.' The owner of the Inn, Glen McGuire was not available for comment. Anyone who may have any information, is urged to contact the Madison County Sherriff's department.*

"Marley."

I looked up from my paper to see Ryan Duff sitting on my doorstep, with a wad of pictures in his hand. "Oh, hi there." For a moment I thought about running away but what good would that do? This entire situation had officially become silly. We were both onto each other, it was time to cowgirl up. I just hated the fact that he had completely caught me off guard, I felt like he was in control in this out of control situation.

"I thought maybe I could catch you after your morning run. You got a minute?"

"Um, yeah. I guess so." Unsure exactly what to say or how to act, I kept a safe distance. "I'm sorry for snooping. I . . . I," I stammered nervously before Ryan interrupted.

"You can't help it. You had a hunch, something struck you as odd about me. Am I warm?"

"Pretty much, yes," I answered him honestly for once.

"Well, I must say that your radar is pretty well on point. You may just have a gift for this stuff after all. There's a reason why you felt suspicious of me and I should explain things. I *can* explain things, is what I meant to say."

I interrupted him this time. "Because of the white car I saw you drive away in the other night. I talked to a witness who actually saw *the* Boogeyman leaving the scene of the crime in a car matching the same description as the one you were driving. It raised a red flag."

"Because of the car I was driving? Do you know how many white four-doors there are in this town—" Ryan stopped himself and regained his cool before he continued, "And, now? Do you still think it was me?" he asked calmly.

"No, I don't. I cleared you because the license plates on your white car are Illinois plates. The Boogeyman's car has Indiana plates."

"Well, I'm glad to know that I'm *cleared*."

"Actually, you're not completely cleared." I crossed my arms and narrowed my eyes. I needed to study his expression as I asked him about the pictures. "Just how long have you been stalking me for?"

Ryan burst out into an unexpected burst of laughter that ended in a coughing fit. "Excuse me?" he asked, as he tried to quit coughing and took a sip of his water bottle.

I was instantly struck by a pang of self-doubt and I knew that I was very wrong about him. But why else would he have those pictures of me?

"Here, I brought these for you. I don't need them anymore." He handed me the stack of photos, held together by a rubber band.

"Well? I mean, why else would you have all those pictures of me? Hidden away in your desk drawer? I mean other than for spank bank material?" I demanded to know the truth and I would not be put off by his laughing fit.

"*Spank bank*?" His laughing fit continued and he held his hands up over his face that had turned five different shades of bright red. "How do you kids come up with this stuff?" he asked rhetorically, shaking his head in disbelief. My last comment had clearly caught him off guard. "Like I told you when we first met, your Uncle Wayne is a good buddy of mine. We watch each other's backs. When he first found out you were going to move in here *all alone*, he was worried about you. Very worried. So . . . he asked me to keep an eye out for you."

I needed to sit down. I couldn't believe my instincts were that far off base. "Alright, well, even if that's true, why all of the creepy pictures? What are you, a private *dick* in your spare time?" I emphasized the word 'dick,' causing us both to laugh a little at that last remark.

"Alright, I'll admit I got a little carried away. It's just that as soon as you moved in here, you were in trouble. Running around with that Cummings guy, you were involved in that murder investigation, I could go on and on. Wayne knew about all of that and he wanted me to do more than just keep an eye out. He wanted me to look over you . . . constantly. Until that whole mess you were in was cleared up. It was kinda fun for me, I'll admit. Although, maybe I got a little carried away with the pictures."

"I see, well . . . I feel like an idiot. I'm sorry, Ryan. I had no idea, Wayne never mentioned anything to me."

"Look, don't be sorry. I can't imagine what I would have thought, if I were in your shoes and I found pictures of me stashed away in your house. Actually, I probably would have liked it," he said, with a big smile.

"I didn't know that Uncle Wayne was so worried about me. I mean, my Dad is the Sherriff. I'm completely safe," I said, trying to convince myself more than anything.

Ryan looked at me with a doubtful expression. "Just think of me as . . . your guardian angel. No more pictures, I promise."

"Guardian angel, huh? I like that." I thought about it and smiled inwardly. It was really quite sweet, actually.

"And just for the record. The white car is my mother's. I just took it into the shop for her that day. It needed new brakes, new tires, and a tune up, so it would pass inspection. I keep begging her to let me buy her something fancier, but she insists that she likes hers just fine. Can I take a look at that? He pointed to the newspaper under my arm. Suddenly, his face became more serious.

"Sure," I said and handed it to him. I watched his expression turn somber as he began to read the headline.

"Crazy, huh?" I asked Ryan, eager to learn why he seemed so curious about the article. When he didn't respond, I felt the need to fill the awkward silence looming between us. "Have you heard about that story?"

"No, I haven't heard about the latest news, but I've known about the story for years." Ryan looked at me, his face as white as a ghost. His mouth seemed to go dry and his hands trembled ever so slightly as I waited on pins and needles for him to explain. "My sister. The last time she was seen alive was on her wedding night."

"Addy? Is Addy Whitmore is your sister?" I asked, in sheer disbelief. Suddenly, my thoughts flashed back to the framed photo on his desk of the pretty young bride. It was a photo of Addy on her wedding day. His beloved missing sister, whose remains were now being poked and prodded on a cold metal table, in a dark sterile room, where everything was draped in white sheets.

"Whitmore was her married name; her maiden name was Duff. How did you know?"

"I just put some puzzle pieces together. You have to go to the FBI and let them know." I cut him off without any further explanation.

Suddenly, out of nowhere a crash of thunder boomed loudly, through the early morning sky and a torrential downpour ensued.

CHAPTER 17

That morning was invigorating for me. I was dotting my ‘I’s and crossing my ‘T’s. I had cleared things up with Ryan, and most importantly, had reassurance of precisely what and who was haunting the Brass lantern Inn. The rest was pretty much out of my hands. I’d put Ryan in touch with my Dad, who would get him in touch with the FBI. Some DNA testing would be done, hopefully the remains would be identified in a timely fashion, and the Duff family would have some closure. Perhaps by giving Addy the proper burial she deserved, it would allow her to leave this world behind, the way she should have seven years ago. How she wound up in the pond was yet to be determined, although it sounded like the husband was the most likely suspect. Where he was now, one could only guess.

I called Glen McGuire and filled him in on my discoveries. He informed me that there was already a more peaceful vibe throughout the hotel. He then informed me that the hotel’s website has gotten more than 1,000 hits in the last twenty-four hours. They were booked solid with reservations until Christmas. I assured him that, if anything, this would be good for business. After the movie Amityville Horror was made in the late seventies, thousands of tourists flocked to Amityville, New York, every year just to get a glimpse of the house and the town where the rumored terrors had taken place. I bet him that his hotel would have the same sort of following and, if anything, he should play up the hauntings.

We made idle chit chat for nearly twenty minutes or so, which was mostly him rambling and me agreeing and urging him along so I could end the call. He asked for my address so he could mail me a check for my help and I insisted that it was not necessary; and that I didn't feel right about accepting payment for a job such as this. Besides, I was sure Weenie's rates would probably be exorbitant enough.

I only had two classes this morning and then I planned on heading down to Springfield, Illinois to stir up some trouble. I had the rest of the day off and I felt like this was as good a time as any to get the ball rolling on my Boogeyman case. It was only a matter of time before he struck again, so I had to work quickly. I needed to do whatever I could to learn about this man. Getting into his head and learning about his past would give me better insight as to what kind of moves he would make next and where he might be hiding.

I kept the top of my convertible up during my three hour drive south on Interstate 55; the rain had not let up since it started this morning. The cars on the highway were moving at a slow pace and I saw a few cars pulled over to the side of the road, waiting for a break in the weather. I charged on and by the time I made it to Springfield, the rain had morphed into a steady drizzle. Springfield boasted Abraham Lincoln in the way that Washington D.C. touted the White House. Everywhere I looked there were statues, plaques, banners, and even buildings, all with 'Honest Abe's' face plastered on them. It was a nice town, similar to Greenbriar in many ways.

As I sat at a red light, I watched as a group of grade school children crossed the street, hand in hand, all wearing their cute little plaid uniforms and holding onto their lunch boxes; with their teacher leading the way. As I waited at the light, I entered the address I found on line for the Long Bridge facility. According to my GPS, I was only a couple of blocks away. I followed the routed area and pulled up to a formidable looking brick building, encompassed by tall gates topped with rows of barbwire and uniformed guards positioned around the perimeter. I had called on my drive down and made an appointment with Max Etherton, Prison Warden. I told the secretary on the phone that I was an investigative journalist with The Sentinel in Greenbriar but left out the fact that I was a nosey twenty-year-old student working for the student paper. I thought it best to keep my vigilante tactics secret, especially when dealing with the warden. This bit of information was good enough for the warden's personal assistant and I promised that I wouldn't take more than ten minutes of her time.

A quick internet search from my phone told me everything I needed to know about the facility. According to the internet, the Long Bridge Psychiatric facility for the criminally insane currently housed 198 male patients. At any given time, there were up to twenty-five patients on trial leave at other units. Most of the incarcerated patients suffered from *severe* mental illness and caustic personality disorders. The majority of patients had been found guilty of heinous crimes against society. We're talking the worst of the worst, next to death row. Even more demoralizing was the fact that the average stay for this crowd was only eight years.

I pulled up to a uniformed officer, who sat behind a small booth in front of the heavy iron gates. The obvious signs of middle age were apparent in the hollow dark spaces beneath his eyes and the flecks of white in his hair and beard. I told him who I was and that Warden Etherton was expecting me. He shot me a baffled look, as if he couldn't believe I was willingly driving my car into Dante's ninth circle of hell.

"You may wanna . . . ahh . . . ya know, cover up a little." He motioned to my outfit with his index finger. "You don't wanna get these guys all riled, if ya know what I mean." He tipped his head a little toward me as he opened up the gate.

I knew exactly what he meant and it had not even occurred to me as I looked down at my short black leather skirt, black platforms, and fuzzy, cropped cream colored sweater. *Oops* . . . I definitely should have considered wardrobe and dressed accordingly. I pulled into a parking space clearly labeled 'visitors only,' I grabbed my gym back from the back seat, and rifled through its contents. Of course, everything was spandex and not much fabric. Not to mention sweaty and worn but I always had an extra pair of sweatpants in my bag, in case of emergencies. I pulled the sweats on, over my legs and yanked down my leather skirt over the sweats, careful not to reveal any skin, just in case there were any pervs watching. I pulled my hair back into a low ponytail at the base of my neck and wiped off any trace of makeup from my face. There. I was officially de-sexed. I threw on a long black raincoat, buttoned it up, and tied the belt tightly around my waist. I made sure that my pen, notebook, and cell phone were all inside my purse.

I was frisked and searched by a rather large woman at the front desk, named 'Officer Karen,' then I was led through a metal doorway, which was prompted open by a loud buzzer. I was then led down a long bleak, grey corridor to an elevator that took me up to the second level. From there, Officer Karen led me down another long hallway with grey tiled floor and grey walls.

A group of several men was walking in a straight line along the opposite wall; they all wore matching prison mandated orange jumpsuits and their hands were shackled in front of them, as they were led by an austere looking officer. I tried not to stare. I kept to myself and didn't make eye contact with any of them. We finally came to an office door, with plaque on the front labeled, 'Warden M. Etherton.' Officer Karen led me inside and informed the Warden's secretary who I was and why I was there. The secretary buzzed the Warden, who walked into the tiny reception area, mere seconds later. Her large presence filled the tiny room.

"I'm Maxine Etherton." She extended a cold hand, barren of any jewelry, and shook mine with a devastating squeeze. Her blond hair was cropped short, her wide frame filled out the grey suit that matched her black tennis shoes. She wasn't overweight, but had a solid, masculine frame. I could tell immediately that she was tough. Her no-nonsense demeanor told me she had no time for anything other than a few quick details. She gave my outfit a quick once over and seemed to pause when she saw my patent leather platforms. I pulled my raincoat around me ever so slightly.

"I'm sorry. I don't have much time. I have a new inmate arriving in about fifteen minutes. If you don't mind, we'll just do the interview right here in the lobby," she ordered, taking one of the two seats. She filled the space easily and crossed her legs together at the ankles.

"Oh, sure. I just have a few questions about an inmate of yours who recently escaped. His name is—"

"Charles Skinner," Warden Etherton cut me off. "Just so we're clear, I will not make any comments regarding his escape or any other related events." She sat up a little bit straighter and brushed off some invisible lint from her skirt. It hadn't even occurred to me that the escape was a negative reflection on the warden, a mark of shame on her career that an inmate escaped on her watch. I didn't dare bring it up again.

"I understand. I had no intentions of asking you about the escape. I just wanted to ask a few questions about Skinner, himself," I confirmed.

"What is it exactly that you want to know?"

"Well, for starters, why was he incarcerated and how long was he here?"

"You mean you don't know?" she asked, a note of sarcasm lingering in her voice. She looked at me rather disapprovingly. "Charles Skinner was incarcerated for killing his parents. He was a minor when it happened, fifteen years old if memory serves. Not only was he a minor at the time but it was determined he was suffering from severe psychiatric disorders as well."

My stomach lurched at the thought of a young teenager brutally murdering his parents. "Can you tell me how he killed them? His parents, that is."

"He strangled them to death. Asphyxiation." She spoke the words dryly, as if she was talking about the weather. The words held no meaning for her, evoked no emotion. Clearly, her career had drained any kind of emotion from her conscious mind, desensitized every membrane, every cell. "What exactly is this about, Miss . . ."

"Parker. I believe that Charles Skinner may be the person responsible for a string of murders and vicious attacks in Northern Illinois. Please forgive me for speculating and I realize that if I'm wrong, this is slander, but local authorities and I believe it to be a very likely possibility. I'm trying to connect the dots before anyone else gets hurt. By finding out more about Skinner . . . about his past . . . it might help me to find him." I looked hopefully at the Warden.

"I still don't understand. Don't you think you're putting yourself in a rather *dangerous* situation?"

"Well, sure, but that's sort of the nature of my job, but it's more than that. It's become personal to me. My friend, Rose, was a victim of Skinner's and she's fighting for her life right now at St. Aidan's hospital, in Greenbriar."

Warden Etherton's features softened up a bit, her sarcasm was no longer detectable. "Your friend . . . will her condition improve?"

“That remains to be seen. The local police are doing everything that they can, but they are understaffed right now and there are just certain things that are best left to a woman to handle . . . don’t you think?” I tried appealing to her feminist side. My intuition usually steered me into the right direction.

“You got that right.” Warden Etherton poked an index finger in my direction and leaned in closer. “And, it’s a man’s world out there. We have to be tough.”

“Amen,” I said, agreeing to everything she was saying and I didn’t stop there. “I mean, look at you, a woman running a male prison. You’re an inspiration.”

“Thank you.” Warden Etherton blushed a little. “I wish everyone saw it that way.” She interrupted herself abruptly, as if something just jogged her memory and she wanted to hurry up and spit it out before she forgot it. “I remember something about him that sort of separated him from the rest. He loved poetry; he loved books. In fact, he was the librarian at the prison library for a short time. He was smart, clever. If you were to just run into him on the street . . . you would never know he was disturbed. He could be quite charming, when he wanted. So charming, in fact, that he conned a guard to help him escape.” She shook her head in utter disapproval, looking down at her hands.

I didn’t push her further on the topic of his escape, but I did ask her where I might find some of his family members. She had no problem giving me the address for Charles’s sister. She was the next stop on my list, which allowed me to kill two birds with one stone. I wanted to talk to her *and* get a look at Charles's old house. We said our goodbyes and parted ways with a mutual respect for the other's profession. She wished me luck and made me promise that I would let her know how things panned out.

The GPS in my car led me easily to 3458 Canterbury Lane, located on the North East side of Springfield, across from the newly renovated town projects. The house was in serious need of some general maintenance. The once white aluminum siding was now a dirty shade of brown; most of it hung loose and looked in serious need of repair.

A large chunk of the roof had obviously been patched up with a plastic tarp by someone without a clue as to what they were doing. All the shrubs and landscaping, which I imagined had been quite lush at some point in time, now stood barren of any greenery. A blue sign was taped to the front door; it was a notice from the local electric company about the power being shut off if they did not receive payment within forty-eight hours of the notice. I was hesitant about knocking on the door, unsure of what I might find on the other side of it. There was no response, so I rang the doorbell next. A frenzied young girl, slightly younger than me came to the door. It looked like she was already on her way out, as she was pulling on her coat and had her keys in hand. She was small, petite, with a wisp of pale blond hair pulled back into a clip. The dress beneath her coat was a white uniform of sorts, with a plastic nametag that read 'Missy.'

"Missy. Hi. Did I catch you at a bad time?"

"Do I know you?" she asked, highly suspicious, as she studied my features and zipped up her coat.

"Not exactly. My name is Marley Parker. I drove all the way down here from the Chicago area, hoping I could talk to you for just a few minutes." It just occurred to me that she probably thought I was a process server or someone from a company coming to turn something off. "Oh, I'm just a college student and I'm doing a little research on your family . . . ehh . . . History." I knew immediately she had heard it all and certainly wasn't about to do me any favors.

"Yeah, sure. You've got reporter written all over you. Go to hell," she said under her breath, as she slammed her front door, locked it and then started to walk away.

"Missy! Wait! Just two minutes."

"I'm late for work. I've gotta get money to pay my damn light bill before they shut me off."

Quickly, I searched in my wallet to see how much cash I had. Twenty-five bucks and a coupon for half off a pair of lace hip-huggers at Victoria's Secret. "Here," I handed her the money and the coupon. "It's yours. I just want a few minutes of your time."

"Like I said, I'm late for work." She turned again and took off at a fast walk down the street. Evidently, she didn't have a car. I had to think of something fast, so I hopped back in my car and drove up next to her on the road. "Wanna lift?" I asked, with a kind smile. "Maybe we could talk on the way?"

Missy stopped and stared at my car and gave me a dramatic roll of her eyes. "Is this really your car?" she scoffed.

"Sort of. It was a gift."

"A gift? What do you do? Turn tricks on the side or somethin'?" she said, as she opened the door and got into the seat next to me.

"Umm...no. I just saved a rich guy's life and I guess he thought he owed me."

"Hmm, nice guy."

"Yeah, well . . . that's debatable . . . Anyway. Where can I drop you?"

"The diner over on Tenth Street. Mind if I smoke?" she asked, after her cigarette was already lit and she was puffing away.

I almost screamed but stopped myself. "Not at all," I lied, and unrolled her window from the electric panel on the driver's side of the car.

"I'm sorry about what happened to you." I spat out the words. I had no idea how to begin this conversation. "I can't imagine what you must have gone through. My mom was killed when I was really young and I'll never be the same person that I would have been, if she were still here. It sucks." Suddenly feeling melancholy, relating to my new source, I said, "Screw it. Can I get one of those too?" I pointed to her box of Camel lights. She smiled ever so slightly and handed me a cigarette and her yellow lighter. I could tell she was starting to warm up to me. That's the thing about people: everyone is apprehensive toward strangers. Something instilled into our brains from day one. *Don't talk to strangers, stranger danger.*

I've never completely felt that way. I mean, obviously, you have to take care not to talk with just anyone, but I always think about that famous line from 'A Streetcar Named Desire,' when Blanche Dubois says, "I've always depended on the kindness of strangers." For some reason, that line always resonated with me, whenever I was trying to derive information from complete strangers. Relying on their help to solve the mystery and complete my story.

"Yeah, you're right it *does* suck." She took another deep drag from her cigarette and grinned to herself.

"Have you been a waitress for very long?"

"About three years now. I dropped out of high school and that was the only thing I've ever been any good at."

"So you enjoy it?"

"I guess I do." Her eyes looked sad and her faced looked older than it should have. I assumed most of it was from the smoking, but I'm sure it was a combination of that and the stress from everything she had been through. "Look," she said, "I don't know where my brother is, if that's what you're wanting to know. I haven't seen him since . . . that night. He escaped from Long Bridge and took off. I don't know where he went, but he ain't in Springfield."

I took a drag of my cigarette and coughed violently. "Sorry. I'm not much of a smoker." This caused Missy to laugh and I laughed at myself too. "I'm not trying to find out where he is . . . well, that's not entirely true. I guess I'm just trying to figure him out a little better. I want to get inside his head. What did he like to do as a kid? Do you have any good memories of him?'

"I have zero *good* memories of that freak. He was always getting into trouble. I remember, once, the neighbors lost their brand new kitten, Angel. A pretty little white fluff ball; they had the whole neighborhood searching for that thing. One night, they went out for a little while. When they came back home, they found Angel, gutted like a fish and hanging from the ceiling fan in their kitchen. It was dangling by a rope that was wrapped around its neck." She shook her head and looked down at her lap, as she fiddled with a loose thread on her coat. "I saw Charlie in his room that night, his clothes and his hands still covered in blood. He was standing in front of the mirror, just staring at himself, smiling, with a knife sticking out of his back pocket. Sick little bastard."

I didn't say anything. I just sat there and did my best to hide my disgust.

"Oh yeah, and the freak loved to hang around graveyards. Sometimes funeral homes too. It was like he was totally obsessed with dead things. He would sit in graveyards for hours and make those gravestone rubs . . . you know what I'm talkin' about?"

"Oh yeah, when you take a crayon with the paper peeled off, then hold a piece of paper up to the stone and rub the crayon over the letters?"

"Yeah, it makes an impression of the headstone. Turn here," she instructed, "and it's the diner two blocks down, on the right." Missy pointed down the road and threw her cigarette butt out the window. She wasn't much for manners or political correctness, but she had a harder life than most could begin to imagine. "He was always reciting poetry, too. He would always make up his own versions though, always about morbid shit."

I pulled in front of the diner and put the car in park. "Thank you. I mean that was actually really helpful. Don't forget this." I handed her the twenty-five dollars and noticed she was staring at my charm bracelet. It only had one charm so far, a beautiful medal of St. Jude.

"Thanks," she said and stuffed the money into her coat pocket. "That real?" She nodded to my silver bracelet.

"Its white gold. That's Saint Jude." I referenced the robed man holding a staff that was centered on the charm. He's the patron saint of lost causes. My Uncle Wayne gave it to me for my birthday; it's his favorite saint.

"My mom used to have one like that," Missy said softly.

Without hesitating, I unhooked the clasp and wrapped it around her wrist. "Here, take it. It'll keep you safe." I squeezed her hand and said, "Take care of yourself."

She looked over at me in disbelief. "Thank you." She smiled at me for the first time, revealing a mouth full of crooked teeth. She stepped out of the warm car and into the chilly air. "Oh, and if you ever find my brother, tell him I want my car back!" She turned again toward the diner.

"Missy, wait! What kind of car?"

"It's a Ford. White, four-door. Nothing special. I didn't report it missing because I figured he's the one who took it."

"Just one more thing . . ." I held up my right index finger and asked, "Random question, but what kind of plates does your car have? Are they by any chance out of state plates?"

"Indiana. I bought it cheap off a neighbor down the road. She'd just moved here from Indianapolis. Why do you wanna know?"

"Just a hunch I had."

CHAPTER 18

Finally, it was Saturday night and I was thrilled about the idea of taking a night off. It was the night of Ryan Huff's big Halloween party, and after the week I'd had, I was in desperate need of some fun. I had already made a last minute trip to the mall, for my costume. I opted for the 'Alluring Angel' in a bag costume for fifty bucks. It came complete with a cheap, white, faux satin dress, halo, and the most obnoxiously large wings I had ever seen.

I spent some time getting ready that night; I wanted to get dolled up. I was in a mischievous mood and I wanted to flirt and dance and throw caution to the wind. I spent about an hour curling my hair in small individual pieces with a curling iron, carefully spraying each piece until I had curled every last strand on my head. I flipped my head upside down, shook out my long curls, and sprayed it again. I applied hot pink lipstick and a thick layer of black mascara to my already full eyelashes, topping them off with a layer of black liquid liner. The effect was more of a centerfold than an angel, but what the hell? It was Halloween. I had no curfew and no date I had to worry about babysitting. I would make friends when I got there and not constantly check the time or my phone for missed calls. The Journalist in me was hanging it up for the night.

I walked over to Ryan's house and took a moment to check out the stars in the black sky. It was so clear I could even see Orion's belt. Even though Ryan just lived next door, there was still quite a bit of distance between our homes. He had a few acres of land that extended along the shoreline. I had never been back there, but only saw it from a distance on my morning runs. I had always noticed his small apple orchard, a rather large boat house or guest quarters, and a dilapidated red barn; situated next to a chicken coop.

I let myself in the front door. The music coming from the band inside was almost deafening. I liked it; it suited my mood. It was classic heavy metal and it drowned out any apprehensions I had about coming here alone. I looked around at the crowd and didn't recognize anyone I knew from behind the masks and face paint. I walked over to the elaborate bar set up in the corner of the large room that looked like all of the furniture had been removed for the party. Every room, every crevice within viewing range, was decked out with some sort of spooky décor. Spider webs covered the ceilings, while a purple strobe light and silver flashing disco ball cast colorful specks across the open first floor. Cleverly carved pumpkins lined the entryway and skeletons hung in front of the picture windows. Old black and white horror movies were being projected onto the massive walls. I pushed my way up to the bar and just as I was about to order a diet coke, I stopped and heard myself ask for a vodka tonic. I would be twenty-one in a couple of months anyway; I doubted anyone would notice. After I grabbed my drink, I walked around the house to admire the decorations and the costumes. I could not believe how completely extravagant this party was. Ryan must have spent thousands just on the open bar and gourmet looking canapés being passed out on silver trays by the wait staff. *The man does not do anything on a small scale, that's for sure.*

"Go big or go home. That's my motto," Ryan said, with a bawdy chuckle. He had bumped into me, or rather, danced into me. Judging by his fangs and hulking black cape, it was safe to assume he was dressed as a vampire.

"Hey there, *Count Duff,* thanks for the invite." I felt a little bit apprehensive, but tried my best to disguise it. I was unsure if I should bring up his sister and that whole situation, but I thought better of it and decided not to. Nothing would get in the way of fun tonight. I noticed a tall blonde walk up to Ryan, carrying a drink for him and one for herself. She wore a matching black cape with a teeny-tiny black leather dress. She had the body of a supermodel, with legs nearly as twice as long as most women's legs.

"Here ya go, honey, Jack over ice." The blonde handed Ryan the drink with a bright smile and I instantly recognized her as the same tall blonde who had been burning dinner in his kitchen the other night.

"Thanks, babe," Ryan addressed his girlfriend and gave her a quick kiss on the cheek. "Marley, this is my girlfriend, Linda." Ryan motioned to the blonde. "Linda, this is my neighbor and new friend, Marley."

Linda gave me a warm smile and we shook hands. We talked for several minutes and got to know each other. It turned out that we both had gone to the same grade school and her Aunt Gladys was friends with my Aunt Cecelia. This was a typical interaction between two strangers meeting for the first time in a town like Greenbriar. It was a big small town, where most everyone could be linked to each other in some way. Before I knew it, we were laughing and exchanging funny stories. She didn't seem to know about the fact that I'd broken into Ryan's house, thank goodness. Just as she was beginning to tell me how she and Ryan met, we were interrupted by another couple, eager to chit-chat with Ryan and Linda.

I had drained the remnants of my vodka tonic and excused myself to go get another drink. At the bar, I ordered yet another vodka tonic, although I was already starting to feel fuzzy from the first drink. I promised myself that I would just sip this one slowly. I saw Linda wave to me from across the room, motioning me to come back. I waved back, alerting her that I was on my way.

I took in the elaborate costumes as I made my way back over to Ryan and Linda. That's what I liked best about Halloween, the costumes. I loved people-watching; loved to see who came up with the most unique and creative costumes. I wondered if there was any other place on the planet as entrenched in this holiday as my hometown. I accidentally bumped into a pink-clad Glenda the Good Witch, arm in arm with another woman dressed as the Wicked Witch of the West. I pushed past and felt someone tap me on the arm. It was Eddie from the dojo, dressed as a beat up boxer. He wore boxing gloves, with an American flag on his shorts. Both of his brown eyes had purple makeup around them, giving the impression of two black eyes.

"Oh my, what big *biceps* you have, Mr. Balboa," I teased him excitedly and laughed, happy to recognize someone my own age. Eddie made muscles, mocking the boxer he came dressed as.

"Rocky's my favorite movie, plus it's a cheap costume." Eddie took a quick drink of his beer and gave me the once over. "You look smokin' hot girl. Damn." Eddie bit his knuckles for effect.

"Stop it . . . You've just never seen me outside of the gym. I know it's hard to believe, but I'm usually quite fancy." I smiled and took another drink of my vodka tonic.

"I'll say." Eddie returned my smile and it just dawned on me that he was flirting.

"So, what are you doing here? How do you know all these *old* people?" I asked Eddie, slightly flirtatiously.

"Linda's my cousin. I think the average age of this party is probably thirty-five, not exactly old." We had developed a witty banter that was quickly becoming more and more flirtatious by the second.

"Point taken. Well, it's my first time here. With an invitation, anyway . . ." My voice trailed off.

Eddie just laughed, "Have I mentioned how hot you look? I mean . . . wow. Like one of those Victoria's Secret angels." Eddie playfully grabbed the tip of one of my wings.

"Something like that." I smiled back. "Well, I've gotta run. I'm actually on my way over to talk to your cousin and her boyfriend."

"Here," Eddie wrapped his arm over my shoulders, "I'll escort you. I can push my way through the crowd like no one else." His bulging biceps and abs of steel proved him to be an imposing force as we shoved our way through the sea of ordinary people cleverly disguised in their innovative costumes. I would never date a muscle head, but I was certainly enjoying the attention and the escort. We barged back into the group conversation, arm and arm, and I laughed at an incredibly stupid joke that Eddie was telling me, even though I don't think he meant it to sound quite that stupid. My laughter was suddenly ground to a halt when I saw the unsettling look in Ryan's eyes. Almost like he was warning me about something or trying to signal me with his eyes. Whatever it was went completely over my head and I heard Linda say, "Marley, I'd like you to meet my friend Brittany and her date. I'm sorry, what was your name again?" Linda asked in a tipsy, absentminded tone.

"Rob Cummings," I said out loud, in a noticeably harsh, flat tone. Rob just stared at me and watched as my smile faded and the color from my face drained from rosy to pale in seconds; all from the mere sight of him. Such a profound effect this man had over me. This man whose father killed my mother, whose life I saved, who vanished without as much as a *goodbye*. No explanation, nothing. He just vanished from my life, leaving me alone to deal with reality and shovel through the endless piles of shit left in his wake.

And now here he was, standing in front of me. Smiling, laughing with another girl. Why wasn't he smiling and laughing with me? It should be me at his side, not dippy Brittany, dressed up like a girl scout. Of course, he wasn't in costume. He was far too cultivated for that type of classless behavior, far too proud of himself as he was, why mask perfection?

My heart stopped beating. It did. It literally stopped beating and I couldn't remember how to breathe. I finally met Rob's eyes and allowed them to penetrate right through me. His face was an indelible vision of beauty and mystique. I immediately became consumed with emotion. In that moment, I felt like all of my necessary bodily functions that were keeping me alive had simultaneously stopped. There was no air in the room. I was frozen, unable to speak or move. I didn't know what to do. I felt the familiar burn of red hot tears prick the back of my eyeballs. *Just RUN! Run*, was the only coherent thought in my mind. So, I did just that. I turned, in slow motion, in a way that felt like I was forcing my body against a heavy current, and took my first step into a sea of creatures all laughing and smiling. I tripped over the train of a long wedding dress, worn by a woman dressed an eighteenth century zombie-bride. I was on the floor and I noticed that I had skinned one of my knees from my fall. Red blood began to drip down my leg and I stupidly began to wipe it off with the palms of my hands. People around me stopped to stare; they whispered, taking in the dramatic situation before them. I had to get out of there before the tears began to roll down my face. Big, ugly, messy; black mascara tinted tears that would ruin my makeup and stain my white dress.

I got myself up off the ground, when Rob scooped a hand around my waist and pulled me up. I pushed him away and took off through the party. I had to push my way through the tight crowd that was beginning to suffocate me. I needed air, a quiet place to think and to cry, alone. Finally, I made it to the back of the house and headed for the French doors off the kitchen, barging through them and running as fast as I knew how. The cold air slapped me in the face with an icy sting, reawakening my senses. I didn't know what to do or how to stop the way I felt about Rob. I hated that I cared so much about him. I wished I didn't; I wished that I could go back to the same, head-strong confident person I was before I'd met him. Instead of always looking over my shoulder or searching through faces in the crowd; looking for him. Always looking for him. His face was forever on the forefront of my conscious mind and no matter how hard I tried, I couldn't shake him.

So, I just kept running. I felt my halo fall to the ground and I shed my heavy white wings like a butterfly sheds its cocoon: my metamorphosis from light to dark. I kicked off my heels and kept running until I couldn't keep the tears at bay any longer. I collapsed between a row of apple trees. I was far enough from the house; I figured it was safe to break down. I fell to the ground. The dirt was soft and the rocks and sticks dug into my knees. The combination of tears and dirt created a muddy mess as I wiped my tears with my fingertips. I was a wreck. I had to stop.

I allowed myself to weep incessantly for a moment—something I should have done weeks ago but couldn't. I cleared my throat, opened my eyes, and got my bearings. I leaned against an apple tree for support. I was standing directly in the middle of a small orchard, about half a football field away from the house. I was at the end of Ryan's property. I must have run all the way into the apple orchard in his yard, as there were rows of apple trees on either side of me. I felt a little dizzy as I stood, trying to decipher East from West, before I could sulk back home.

I couldn't seem to shut off the tears. Once they came; they were uncontrollable. I continued to wipe them from my face once again, and then wiped my hands onto my dress. I felt a sharp sting from my skinned knee and noticed that the blood had continued to drip down my leg. I couldn't feel much of anything, with all the adrenaline and vodka that was pumping through my body. I couldn't have cared less at that moment that my white costume was destroyed from the red blood, the tears, and the dark mud from my hands as it rubbed off onto the white silk of my costume. I couldn't resist the perfectly round red apple that hung from a branch, right in front of my nose. I studied the apple and the tree it grew from momentarily before I plucked it from the branch. The vibration from the rattling branch sent crows fleeing and cawing into the cold night. That's when Rob appeared. I didn't say a word, but stared up at him guilelessly. Part of me knew he would come find me and maybe another part of me wanted him to. I noticed he was carrying my wings under one arm and my halo in his hand. I allowed him to come closer. Closer again. Just close enough for me to clench my fist and punch him in the face. And I did. Hard.

His reaction surprised me, as I expected him to be livid, possibly even retaliate. Instead, he briefly closed his eyes and flinched as he tried to conceal any sign of pain, although the strength of my punches had been known to make grown men fall to their knees at the dojo. He grabbed hold of my forearms tightly and pulled me in close to him. The closest I had been to him, outside of my dreams. His scent, his touch, was all too real. I was mere putty in his hands.

"Hell of a right hook you got there," he grumbled, with clenched eyelids and his mouth closed tightly into a funny smirk, with a little tremor of his head as he shook off the pain.

I felt the familiar energy radiating from him and felt the familiar leap of my heart-rate as it began to sky rocket out of control. I didn't say a word. There was too much left unsaid between us, so much that needed to be cleared up, but now was not the time. Instead, we just stared at each other. He looked at me in a way that I had never been looked at before. Almost like the way I had looked at the apple I had just picked. In his eyes, I was ripe, juicy, and ready to be devoured.

A fleeting thought crossed my mind: I always wondered what I would do or say to Rob when I saw him again. I had all these wild fantasies about saying the perfect words that would haunt him for the rest of his life—the life that I had saved from an unimaginable death. Maybe I would scream at him, attack him, and curse at him, spit on him. But now that I was face to face with him and the moment had *finally* presented itself out of nowhere . . . I couldn't bring myself to do any of those things. I was frozen. It's always easy to say, 'I would never.' I would never kiss him again; I would never give him a second chance. But the truth is: You should never say never because you never know what you will do when actually in that imagined situation. And yet here I was. I wanted to love him. Hurt him. Possess him. Bewitch him. So I told myself it was okay. Just go with my feelings for once. What was I waiting for anyway? At that moment, I shut reason out and allowed myself to fall.

And fall, I did. I could actually feel it happening. We seemed to move toward each other at the same time, as we began kissing one another hungrily. We were suddenly attacking each other like two people who had been stranded in a dry desert for days and had come across a body of water. It quickly got out of control from there.

He pushed me back against an apple tree, taking in my entire face with his kisses. The bark from the tree began cutting into my back and burning, so I grabbed him and shoved him backward, pinning him up against a tree. Suddenly I was the aggressor, hungry for more. Insatiable. He bit my lip mid-kiss and I tasted blood, so I bit him back, until I tasted his blood. He grabbed me once more, and impetuously threw me on the ground. Much to my chagrin, I didn't object, but allowed my hands to clumsily caress the well-formed muscles on his arms. He was so strong.

But so was I. Asserting my strength once more, I flipped him over and now I was straddling him. I lifted the white dress over my head and slowly wrapped it around his wrists, until they were bound together securely. I looked him in the eyes and still couldn't bring myself to speak any words. I leaned in again to kiss him playfully this time, breathing him in. I tasted the metallic blood from his lip. Then I licked the sweat and the mud from his cheek in one slow, fluid motion. From his lips all the way up to his forehead. I was no longer myself but a wild girl, scared of nothing. And then something peculiar happened. Something unexpected.

Out of nowhere, I had a fleeting daydream of Rob's father as a drunken co-ed. One hand on the wheel, the other lifting up a bottle of liquor to his lips, his coal black hair flowing back in the breeze without a care in the world. Laughing while he turned up the volume on the car stereo, then the sudden jolt he must have felt when his car suddenly collided with something in the road. Someone. My Mom. I stopped. I looked at him blankly, crossed my arms over my bare chest, suddenly wanting to conceal myself. I stared at him one last time, taking a visual snapshot of his vulnerable face before I stood up and walked away.

CHAPTER 19

I woke up the next morning to tears already in my eyes even before they were opened. My bottom lip was swollen and I could taste the dried blood caked on the edges. My back felt like it was on fire. I gently ran my fingertips over the delicate skin and felt the deep scratches from the tree and from Rob. My fingertips found the remnants of mud, stuck to various parts of my body. I reached my hand up to wipe the hair out of my eyes and ended up with a handful of dirt and leaves. I fished the debris from my long locks. *What the hell was I thinking?* I asked myself, as the loud chirp of the doorbell forced me to sit upright in my bed and face reality. I looked across by bedroom into the mirror directly across from me.

"You have got to be kidding me," I said out loud, frightened at my own reflection. My hair was a tangled, gnarly mess and I had mud and mascara all over my face. I looked down at my hands and they had dark crimson streaks of blood over them and underneath my fingernails. "Ahhh!" I let out a faint little scream at the blood, but then my mind flashed back to the cut on my arm from the tree branch. Wait a minute . . . was I . . . Naked? How could I have forgotten? I'd left my costume tied around Rob's wrists . . . Wow, some night.

The doorbell rang again. Quickly, I stepped out of my bed but my foot was tangled up in the sheet, which caused me to fall forward, directly on my face. I let out a pathetic howl as I tried to untangle myself from the knotted bed-sheet. I hobbled to the door, with the duvet wrapped tightly around my body like a towel.

"What the hell happened to you?" Ryan Duff's terse tone was sobering beyond words. "It looks like a murder scene in here." He looked at me, dumbfounded, as he made his way inside. "Seriously, were you attacked?"

"Uhhh, no." I rubbed my eyes and wet my lips. I needed water, lots of water. "Not really. More like I was the attack*er*." I wrapped the duvet tighter around me and brushed the hair out of my eyes. "Church this morning, definitely church. You interested?" I muttered.

"I never miss Sunday mass. Besides, it looks like you could use a little holy water. No. Make that a lot of holy water. At least a gallon or so."

Then I noticed he was carrying my angel wings under his arm.

"Oh, I almost forgot," he said. "I came by to give you your wings. Not that I'm so sure you deserve them anymore," he added with a smile. "Maybe a pitchfork would have been more fitting?"

"Alright, alright, I get it." I couldn't help but laugh, even in my current state. I suppose this was a rather humorous scenario. "Let's just say, for once in my life, I allowed myself to loosen up and now I'm feeling very strange about the whole thing. That's all I'm going to say. Oh, and one last thing . . . I'm never drinking alcohol again. Ever, ever again." I looked up at him with raised eyebrows and a shit-eating grin.

"Yeah, but it was fun, wasn't it?" he asked rhetorically, with an all too well knowing glance.

I couldn't answer as I recalled . . . I quivered at the flashback of my nails scratching down Rob's back. I gave a shake and made myself focus on the moment at hand. "St. Jude's has a 10:00 mass." I looked down at my watch, seeing it was already 9:48. "Why don't you meet me outside? I need to get dressed and then we can go beg for forgiveness together. You don't exactly look all that innocent either." I smirked at him.

Ryan and I made it to church half way after the mass had started. We took an inconspicuous seat in the back row. I'd grown up attending mass every Sunday in this church. It still looked the same. The giant gold altar with Jesus Christ nailed to the gold cross in the middle, surrounded by the saints and apostles. Colorful flowers adorned the round carpeted altar. I tried my best to listen to the remainder of Father Martinez's homily without letting my mind fall back to Rob. He was preaching about respecting your body and reminding us that "our bodies were temples of the Holy Spirit and should be treated as such." I felt a sharp nudge from Ryan and a slight laugh escaped my lips.

I looked around and saw families sitting together. Mothers trying to keep their children quiet for the remainder of the homily. I noticed some familiar faces, my Father not being one of them, Thank God. I wasn't sure how I would explain this one. I watched the little old ladies kneeling as they silently recited their rosaries. The familiar smell of incense reminded me of Christmas Eve masses past and I had the overwhelming desire to drop to my knees and pray. What had I gotten myself into this time? I was in deep. I needed clarity. Forgiveness. I prayed for both.

Out of the corner of my eye, I noticed Ryan watch me curiously as I prayed and he seemed to mimic my motions. Awkwardly, he knelt down next to me, his long legs unknowingly sticking out from behind the back of the bench. He folded his hands together in prayer and bowed his head. It was quite clear what I was asking forgiveness for, but what about him?

CHAPTER 20

My phone rang that night, long after I had fallen asleep. The shrill ring harshly sliced through my peaceful nocturnal world, like a stab from a butcher knife. Somewhere in the distance, I could hear the lonely cry of an owl. The clock next to my bed informed me that it was 3:09 AM. My caller ID read 'Doc' and I knew immediately something was wrong.

"Marley. I'm sorry to call at this hour, but I have some bad news."

"Huh?" I cleared my throat, jolted out of bed, and rubbed my eyes. "What? What happened?"

"There was another attack tonight on campus. This time it was one of ours."

"What do you mean, one of ours?" I held my breath, praying it wasn't anyone I knew.

"Her name was Katie Gleeson. Did you know her? She was a senior in the Journalism program. Beautiful, bright girl."

"Wait a minute, why are you referring to her in the past tense? Is she alright? Is she in critical care? I need details!"

"She wasn't as lucky as Rose. She's dead. It's too early to tell, but Officer Cooper said it looked to him like she had been strangled. No other visible bruises or signs of abuse. She was just found about an hour ago by campus police. She was sitting in her car, which was found sitting on the side of the road with her hazard lights on—"

"Just like the others," I interjected.

"Marley, I'm not quite finished."

"There's more?"

"Well, something ever so disconcerting, really. Are you near a computer? Indulge me for just a moment, if you will."

"Yes, I sleep with my laptop; let me just fire it up."

"Good. Now, I want you pull up an internet search site: click on an 'images,' search and enter the name "Katie Lynn Gleeson Greenbriar, Illinois."

I did as I was instructed, suddenly feeling charged full of energy, like an electrical pulse reaching out from my core and exiting through my fingertips. "Okay. There are about six or so pictures in the first row of a beautiful girl. I don't recognize her, if that's what you were wondering." I cut Doc off before he could answer as I clicked on the first picture on the page to enlarge it. "Oh my gosh . . . she looks a little familiar . . . bright smile, long light brown hair down to her chest, green eyes, thin . . ." Suddenly, I realized why Doc wanted me to look at her picture. It sounded like I was describing myself. We could be sisters.

"Do you feel like you're looking in a mirror?" He interrupted my rambling.

"Yeah . . . I sure do."

"That's not all. Guess what kind of car she drives?"

"A red convertible?" The words left my lips slowly as fear took hold of me once again.

"Looks like somebody's on to you."

CHAPTER 21

That night, Jade came over to my house, where we proceeded to dress rather . . . well . . . slutty, really. Ready to put our plan into action, Jade thought it would be best if we dressed the part. I think this was mostly just her idea of having fun and playing dress-up, like we were little girls. Fuchsia agreed to come over and help us. What we didn't bargain for was the full make up, hair, and costumes carefully selected and applied by Fuchsia. She curled our hair, teased it, and sprayed it with an overpowering amount of hairspray. Our makeup matched; we both had fake black eyelashes, heavy black liner, way too much bronzer, sparkling purple shadow, and hot pink lips. We decided our best chance to catch the 'Boogeyman' was to use ourselves as bait. We planned on driving around campus and the surrounding areas first, seeing as though that was where he had attacked two other women.

"Be careful, my darling girls. And remember, Mommy's on standby if you need her. I'll be here, waiting, with the phone in my hand. One more time, what is the emergency text code?" Fuchsia asked dramatically. She gave her pink wig a fluff with her bedazzled blue-tipped nails.

"STUART STICKELMAN. Got it," Jade said with a smile. Stuart Stickelman was Fuchsia's real name before she legally had it changed to Fuchsia Darling.

"Ohhh!! You girls are *bad*. Just the way I like ya. Now go make mommy proud," Fuchsia shouted after us. She made a snapping motion with one hand and held her martini in the other.

I decided it would be best to start out prowling through cemeteries—not exactly my idea of fun but according to Missy, that's where her brother liked to hang out. *Freak-show.* We started off at Hillcrest cemetery, followed by Oakmont cemetery, and finished up at Camp Wheeler cemetery. Jade was quickly losing patience and dying of boredom, so I suggested that we check out the campus, seeing as though this is where two girls had been attacked.

So we began trolling Greenbriar U's campus in my red Mercedes convertible. If the car didn't draw attention, the makeup would. Jade's favorite band, The Black Keys, blared from the car's foreign sound system, also drawing more attention to us. I briefly wondered why he chose the campus as his hunting grounds. Maybe the Boogeyman wasn't Charles Skinner at all but secretly some sort of professor from Greenbriar University with an alter ego; a real Jekyll and Hyde type. The simplest explanation was that he liked young, pretty women. And where better to find them than on a college campus, filled with dark corners and dormitories that housed an abundance of young, pretty girls. Before I knew it, one hour turned into two hours and the Black Keys morphed into the Rolling Stones. Campus was somewhat small, sprawled out maybe six miles maximum. We got tired of driving in circles so we decided to pull over on the side of the road. The cold weather forced us to put the convertible top back up. Jade and I had more than enough time to chat about boys, clothes, school, and Grannie Annie's latest boyfriend 'Mikey', who was at least twenty years her junior.

"So, a thought just occurred to me," Jade said. "Why would the Boogeyman still be driving around campus in his white car, if the police know what kind of car he drives?" She pulled a stray blonde curl from her face. "I mean, isn't that a little risky?"

"Well, that's actually an excellent question. To tell you the truth, I don't think the police have a clue what he drives."

"And how is it that you know and the police don't?" Jade looked over at me suspiciously.

"You don't need to worry about that. Just sit there and look pretty."

"Sonya Ford?' she asked knowingly. "Boy, that Sonya's one clever little minx."

"Believe it or not, I left Sonya out of it. I used a different name to get that information. Like I said, you don't need to know.'

"It's getting late and I have an Organic Chem test in the morning. You can come home and we can put on our pizza pants and have a scary movie marathon," Jade suggested—or more like insisted.

"Throw in some popcorn and you've got a deal. Should we stop by the video store on the way home?"

"You're in."

Half an hour later, Jade and I walked out of the video store, hands full of horror movies, a container of microwaveable popcorn, and two diet cokes. I was right in the middle of revealing the punch line to my new favorite joke that I'd heard from Cat last week. "So, this guy walked into his therapists office butt naked, wrapped in cellophane; and the therapists says, "Clearly I can see your *nuts*." Get it? *Nuts*?'

Jade seemed to mull over the joke for a few seconds, as if she didn't quite get it or she just didn't find it as humorous as I did. "O.M.G. . . . Do you see what I see?" she asked. A look of alarm had suddenly washed over her.

"What did I miss?" I asked, confused. I looked around the parking lot, trying to figure out what she was looking at. I spotted a white four-door sedan, unmarked, with tinted windows and a single overhead light positioned on the roof—the portable type that can be easily placed on the roof in emergency situations. It was the exact description of the Boogeyman's car. The car was parked directly across the street from the video store, in a deserted parking lot that used to house an old book store, a tanning salon, and a small Mexican restaurant.

The driver's side window was slowly rolled up before I could get a look at the driver. I nudged Jade in the side with my elbow and she reciprocated so hard it almost knocked me over. My jumbo diet coke slipped from my hand and splattered onto the concrete, the splash of the icy drink hitting my legs caused me to involuntarily flinch.

"Get back in the car, Jade," I calmly instructed her, as I felt perspiration slowly begin to form on my forehead.

"What the hell are you doing?" Jade asked, as I slowly pulled my convertible across the street and into the abandoned lot across from us. "Seriously, Marley? Are you nuts? I mean this is a little different than the pervy school janitor who liked to steal underwear and shoelaces from the girls' locker room. This guy is a psycho-killer!" she protested, immediately uneasy. I ignored her and took a careful look at the license plates as we pulled up right next to him.

"Did you see that? Indiana plates. *This is our guy*!" I unrolled both of our windows and waved to him. I waited for what seemed like hours before again waving and motioning for him to unroll his window.

"Marley!" Jade whispered, grabbing onto the sides of her seat now, bracing herself for the horror of what she was about to see.

I ignored her as the black window in the adjacent car slowly unrolled. My heart began to beat faster inside of my chest. I was expecting some maniac with wild curly hair, crazy eyes, and crooked teeth. The man next to me seemed to be reasonably handsome. Maybe this was the wrong car and this man really was an undercover police officer. But then again, maybe it wasn't him at all . . . Just as I flipped my hair and plastered on my brightest smile, the white vehicle pulled away. I heard the tires squeal as he pulled off, leaving us in his wake. Jade and I exchanged glances.

"That . . . was . . . creepy," I said slowly.

"We must have scared him off. Should we follow him?" Jade asked. She was somewhere between frightened and energized.

"I've always wanted to try that."

I tried keeping a safe distance behind the suspect as I followed him through town. His speed and pace were erratic. He bounced in and out of lanes the way a ball bounces around a pin-ball machine. As we approached downtown Greenbriar, the traffic became undeniably more dense. On the corner of Eleventh Street and Ivy Avenue, the railroad crossing arms began to lower from their hinges, closing off the street. The white car blew right between the arms before the space between them became too narrow to pass through, leaving me stuck behind the tracks, trapped. I made a loud guttural sound of exasperation and banged my fists on the steering wheel in fury. I watched the raucous Amtrak train as it crossed the tracks in front of us, drowning out every other sound in the night air.

"Oh, well," Jade said calmly. "What would we have done if we did catch up to him? Make a citizen's arrest? This was really a dumb idea." She shook her head, annoyed.

"Dumb? Really? Not to me. We could have followed him . . . Oh I don't know, perhaps found out where he's living or maybe we could have even followed him as he hunted down his next *victim.* Now, I've got nothing on him." As the light turned green, I took off and headed straight for home. It was getting late and it was getting cold. A part of me looked forward to replacing my hooker heels and with my bunny slippers.

Jade's cell phone ringer broke the silence between us. I knew instantly it was Tones calling because I heard the familiar sound of 'the good, the bad, and the ugly' ringtone play from her phone. Jade put the call on speaker so we could all talk.

"How was the movie?" I heard my dad's familiar husky growl on the other end of the line. I had almost forgotten that Jade told a minor fib and led Tones to believe that we were at a movie.

"Hey Pops . . . it was sad...very sad," I stammered as I made something up and Jade glanced at me confused.

"Yeah, the bad guy got away at the end," Jade said and looked at me with a sardonic smile.

I was about to reply with something inane when I saw cherries in my rearview mirror. A white four-door sedan with a single, solitary red flashing overhead police light. No siren. "Dad, we'll call you right back . . . uhh . . . Jade has another call," I said quickly, before I hit the 'end' button on Jade's cell.

She looked at me curiously.

"We've got company," I said, in a matter of fact tone.

"OHHH . . . MY . . . GOSH!" Jade enunciated dramatically. "What do we do now?"

"Okay. Are you ready to put our plan into action?"

"I don't think it's such a good idea. This is scary, Marley. Maybe we should just keep driving . . . Like straight to the police station," Jade replied, as she double checked to ensure that her mace was in her pocket.

"Jade, those girls had no clue what they were getting themselves into by pulling their cars over. They were unarmed and unaware. We know what we're doing and we're armed. Come on!"

"Okay, you're right. I've got the Taser." She looked across the car at me, unsmiling and dead serious.

"Taser gun from Matty, check. Mace from Granny Annie, check. A huge set of balls, check."

"I'm texting Fuchsia now. Just in case," Jade said. "I'll text her the exact location of where we are pulling over. If I don't text her or call her back within five minutes, she will immediately call the cops, directing them to our exact location."

"Alright, good. Foolproof," I assured myself and took a deep breath in. "Now, where should I pull over?" I asked her, equal parts nervous and excited. My mouth was so dry my lips were sticking to my teeth. I embraced the familiar surge of adrenaline and allowed it to wash over me.

"Turn here," Jade instructed, and I turned ahead, down a darkened road without any businesses or houses in sight. I followed the road for about two more minutes, with the Boogeyman still hot on my tail.

"How about over there?" Jade pointed to the large expanse of cornfields about a block ahead of us. "It's the perfect place for a homicidal maniac to slice us into pieces."

"Here goes nothing," I said sarcastically and made a quick sign of the cross as I slowly pulled the car over. We sat and waited, still in our seats. Neither one of us spoke, only watched and listened to the silence around us with the acuity of wolves. We both needed to utilize every ounce of our senses right now. We *had* to outsmart him. We'd gotten ourselves into this, now we had to see it through. There was the only one way out and it involved facing our fears head on, but we would be saving the lives of his future victims. We could do this. Our plan was foolproof. I let my mind momentarily wander back to Rose and the state of her current condition. This animal had to pay. He had to be stopped, once and for all. I had no idea what was taking so long. Was he waiting for us to get out of the car first? I peeked into my rearview mirror and saw a dark figure slowly emerge from the white sedan. My heart rate sped up and I felt cold and light as I allowed the steady stream of adrenaline continue to surge through my veins. My hands and feet felt prickly.

I took a closer look in the rearview mirror. He moved at a steady, slow pace, as he made his way to my convertible. His pale skin glowed like a mask in the dark. His hair was dark and disheveled. It looked like he was wearing some sort of a service uniform. It could easily be mistaken for a police uniform, even an auto mechanic. Vague and dark. Baggy, with long-sleeves and dark boots. I watched carefully in my rearview mirror as he made his way closer to my car. Never had I been so frightened in all my life.

"Marley. Do something." Jade spoke in a hushed whisper next to me, awakening me from my stupor. What I really wanted to do was just come out and ask him: What does it feel like to be such a vile person? Such a waste of air. Were you born evil or was it a personal choice? Does it feel good to hurt helpless women? What is wrong with you?

I started to freak out. To hell with the plan: I wanted to jump through the window and beat him within an inch of his life and leave him for dead on the road. Maybe someone would take pity on him and assume he was road kill. A dead deer, in the dark of night, it was hard to tell out here with no street lights. He would eventually get hit by a car and put out of his misery.

My eyeballs nearly popped out of my head and my breath caught in my chest. I had forgotten how to breathe. "Screw this," I yelled bitterly.

I couldn't sit here waiting any more, pretending to be a helpless victim. I didn't have the patience. I waited until he was right up against my door; pointing his flashlight into my car. Police persona intact. I grunted wildly, as I thrust open the heavy car door with both hands. It surprised him, catching him unaware as I slammed his entire lower body and watched as he bent over in pain. This provided a momentary distraction, but I knew it would only be a matter of seconds before he was upright and on the offensive.

"Jade! Call the police. Now!" I screamed over to Jade as I got out of the car and clumsily removed the mace from my pocket. Without hesitation, I sprayed it all over his face. It was too dark to see much, other than shapes and shadows. I heard the man make a groaning sound as he popped right back up and wiped off his eyes with his shirt sleeve. He didn't utter a single word to me, which only made him less human-like.

The mace didn't seem to faze him even a little. That was fine; I still had the Taser gun.

He jumped up so quickly, I didn't see it coming. At a supersonic speed, he had pinned me up against the driver's side of my car and held my hands behind my back.

I went limp and pretended to have given in. Jade was still seated in the car, frantically texting to Fuchsia or the police, I wasn't sure. This allowed me to make eye contact with her and shout the word 'TASER.' She had it in her hand, ready to deliver.

I stomped down hard on his right foot with my stiletto heel, which loosened his grip around my wrists, and then I popped my butt back toward him; shoving him hard directly in the pelvis. That allowed me to grab the Taser gun from Jade. I quickly turned and tasered him right in the face. This did not exactly have the effect I had anticipated, as he only stood in shock and pain for a mere moment before grabbing a strong hold of my hair with one hand and putting me in a choke hold with the other.

Jade came flying out of the car with her baseball bat. What was she doing? She couldn't take him on. In my peripheral vision, I watched her race around the car. She swung the bat like a pro, aiming right for his back. I heard something make a cracking sound, but he didn't seem to notice much. It was odd, it was like he couldn't feel pain. He was just cracked hard in the back with a bat, tasered in the face, and maced. He should be doubled over in pain, begging for mercy. Instead, he seemed angrier and stronger than before.

Still holding onto my hair, he let go of my neck so he could defend himself from Jade. Just as Jade was about to take another swing with her bat, he grabbed it right out of her hands and tossed it into the distance; it landed somewhere in the vast field of corn. So, I made an abrupt aikido move: Tachiwaza-mae. In other words, I attacked him front the front with a punch to the face and kick in the balls.

"RUN JADE!! GO! Run for your life," I yelled into the night air, praying that she would listen to me for once.

Jade didn't argue; she just took off into the cornfields on a sprint. *Good girl.* His chances of finding her in the dense fields were slim, if she just kept running. I should have never involved her. What was I thinking? I never *actually* thought we'd make it this far, never fully believed that we would run into him.

I now realized how pathetic my idealistic expectations were, of what would happen tonight. I hadn't thought this through properly and now Jade's life was in danger. It was just a hare-brained scheme I'd created on a whim. *Stupid was a good word for it.*

I looked up at him. His eyes were blank. Two black empty holes, like staring into the depths of hell. There was only one thing left in my bag of tricks . . . Stall.

"I'm sorry," I said. "You're just . . . so strong. I never should have come at you like that." He just stood there, motionless—a cold heavy statue. One false move on my part and he wouldn't hesitate to snap the fragile vertebral bones in my neck, which would shoot up into my brain, causing instant death.

The icy talons of fear ripped through my body, as cold as ice. I knew what I had to do. I had one card left to play and it had to be convincing or he would kill me. *This was it. My one shot. I better make it good.*

I playfully traced the lines on his face with my finger before I felt my fingertip trace over the gaping scar across his cheek. There was no question. He was Charles Skinner. I stood on my tip-toes, just high enough to reach his mouth. Every nerve ending tingled as I tried desperately to keep my fear at bay.

"If I knew you were this good looking," I gave a sexy little laugh, "I wouldn't have been so. . . so, mean before," I whispered softly and close to his face. He just stood there, observing me. One false move and I was dead. I knew I had no other choice, as I placed my mouth over his and slowly kissed him. Gently at first, and then more passionately.

His lips were cold. Rough and unresponsive. I realized that he wasn't kissing me back. I tried my best to get him into a vulnerable position so that I could attack him again. If I could do that, then maybe I could buy myself enough time to run into the fields with Jade. He was still holding onto a chunk of my hair at the base of my scalp. His grasp was so strong, I could already picture a bloody bruise beginning to swell on my head. Then I heard a wicked little chuckle escape from his lips.

He never spoke a word. Even with the glow from the full moon, I could only make out vague facial features. His skin was pale, scarred. He had two dark holes for eyes. He could have been wildly handsome or even hideously disfigured and I wouldn't have been able to tell the difference. This was not good. I knew that if he wasn't afraid to show me his face, then he wouldn't hesitate to kill me. What did it matter if a dead girl saw his face? Who would she tell?

I'd thought I was scared before, but it was nothing compared to this moment. I had done everything I could think of and it still wasn't enough. Without thinking, I took my right thumb and shoved it back into his eyeball. He tried to pull my hand away but it was too late. The damage had been done and I had a firm grip with my right hand, as I used the hard bone of his eye socket to support myself. I continued to push the soft, gooey, gelatinous ball all the way into the back of his skull. He howled and moaned in pain. *Finally*, he felt something. I was beginning to worry I had lost my touch.

My long fingernails clawed, scraping and gouging away any inner parts that may still be vital to his eyesight. He howled and moaned. I yanked my thumb away and didn't allow myself to vomit from the sensation of the slimy mucus and bloody matter that now covered my hand and slid down my arm like a warm ooze. I refused to let it get the best of me and I knew this would be my last opportunity to escape. While he was still doubled over in pain, I made a roundhouse kick to his head, which caused him to collapse into a heap on the ground. I ripped my high heels off of my feet and hurled them at his limp body before I ran into the cornfield.

I kept telling myself to run. It became more difficult with every step. The sharp edges of debris and corn stalks that lay on the ground dug into the naked soles of my feet as I ran fervently, deeper into the corn. I could feel beads of sweat forming on my nose, despite the chilly night air. The corn must have been at least ten feet tall. I always remembered my Dad telling me that if I ever needed to hide from someone, to run into the cornfields. I continued to run through the tall dry corn, as I did my best to make a confusing zigzag route, lessening the likelihood of being found.

I stood still for a moment. The deafening silence was almost eerie, in a way, until finally, a cold breeze swept through the field, rustling through the leaves and rattling the stalks. The only light was the soft glow from the stars and full moon. It felt like I had been standing there for an eternity, but realistically had only been about forty seconds or so. I wondered if Jade was having any luck getting a cell signal. I found it easier to tell myself that she had and police would be here in a matter of minutes.

I came to a sudden stop in front of an old combine parked just a few feet away. It looked as if the farmer had stopped harvesting the fields and had left it parked there until he could finish up, as October was typically the month for the annual reaping.

I headed further in behind the tractor, but I tripped over an inanimate object on the ground.

"Marley! SHHH! It's me!" Jade whispered loudly, as she squatted on the ground next to the tractor; curled into a ball, with her head down and her back acting as a shield protecting her vital organs from any damage.

“That’s the position you crawl into when you’re shielding yourself from a hurricane, moron!” I whispered back to her. My mood suddenly elevated, knowing I was successful at half blinding the Boogeyman and I had found my sister safe and sound.

“Shut up! Who the hell cares? We’re about to become soil! Where’s the psycho?” she asked, remaining in her position. I noticed she still had her high heels on and I wondered how she had managed to keep from breaking something.

“I blinded him! In one eye, anyway. Oh, and I kissed him.”

“Huh?” she asked, confused, as she looked at me like I was the psychopath.

“It wouldn’t be the first psycho I’ve kissed.”

“Probably won’t be the last either,” Jade said, her tone matter of fact. “Let’s just lay low until the cops get here.”

“I don’t think we have any other options,” I whispered back to her.

“I wouldn’t be so sure about that,” Jade said smugly, as she tossed me a lightweight set of keys. She shot an exaggerated look up at the tractor. “The keys were in the ignition!”

“You are *brilliant*!” I felt a momentary wave of relief wash over me. This was our getaway. Our safe house, our refuge. Our silver lining to this night from hell.

“Do you know how to work this thing?” I asked her.

“Why would I know how to drive a tractor?” Jade’s whisper was progressively becoming a yell.

Before we could argue, we both saw headlights off in the distance, coming from the main road.

"Come on! It can't be that hard!" I whispered to Jade and pointed to the tractor in front of us.

With the agility of foxes, we both hopped inside the tractor like we had done it a million times before. We made a good team. This positioned us much higher than the corn, giving us a far better vantage point than before. The darkness worked against us, as it was still nearly impossible to see further than right in front of us. My eyes frantically searched for the ignition.

"Here!" Jade whispered, as she pointed to what appeared to be the ignition. I shoved the key in and turned.

If the Boogeyman didn't know where we were hiding before, he did now. I was shocked at how loud the rumble of the engine was. "Now what?" I screamed to Jade.

"Just start pushing buttons!" she yelled back at me. So, without any idea of what we were doing, we both frantically pushed every knob, pulled every lever, and turned every dial we encountered on the dash. The formidable machine began to make peculiar sounds, as different moving parts were now working in action together. Every part but the headlights, which I wasn't even sure were standard in combines such as this.

Music began screaming from somewhere, which caused both Jade and I to jump simultaneously. Jade gave a little scream. It took me a minute before I understood that it was coming from a speaker somewhere in the combine. I think it was the Moody Blues, 'I Know

You're Out There Somewhere.*' How very apropos,* I thought to myself.

Jade and I looked at each other curiously as we listened intently to the Moody Blues song lyrics; *'I know I'll find you somewhere. Somewhere, somehow. Somewhere in your wildest dreams . . . '*

"Great song," I agreed, and began to sing in a hushed whisper along to the words . . . *'Somehow I'll return again to you . . .* ' I gently pushed down on what I assumed was the gas pedal and the tractor jerked ahead so forcefully that Jade almost fell out of it. I didn't know how to stop it; it just kept propelling forward. I stepped on another pedal, assuming it would stop but it only caused it to go faster. It felt like there were four or five pedals in total and I hadn't a clue which was which.

"You okay?" I yelled over to Jade.

"Fine! Keep going!"

I looked around us. It was hard to see anything other than corn flying. "Let's try to use this thing to get us out of here!"

I continued to plow forward. It felt like I was making some progress in finding my way out of this field, but I couldn't be certain. That's when I heard the sirens and saw the flashing red lights.

"They're here!" I yelled joyfully. I took my foot off the gas and turned the engine off. Without the tractor decimating the corn and roar of the engine, I was finally able to get my bearings. We were close enough to the road to jump out of the tractor and sprint toward the police cars. I felt that we were finally safe. Jade and I both jumped down and sprinted back to the road, where we saw four police cruisers and Fuchsia's purple Volkswagen.

"Over there! I see them!" I heard Fuchsia yell to the police, as she honked her horn and flashed her brights, trying to get our attention as Jade and I made it safely up to the main road.

"Where is he?" I shouted to the officers. "Did you catch him?" I asked hopefully, but I already knew the answer. The Boogeyman was gone. Disappeared into the night, probably forever. My big plan to catch him now seemed pitiful and stupid. He was too many things. Too strong, too fast, and too smart. My heart felt like it dropped down to the floor of my stomach when I saw my Dad step out of the Sheriff's cruiser. The look on his face seemed to be one more of concern rather than anger.

"Come here, you two," he said, with a look of exasperation. Jade and I obeyed and both fell straight into his arms. "What the hell am I gonna do with you boys?" he asked and squeezed us in a little tighter.

"I'm sorry, Daddy. It was a stupid idea. I never should have gone after him on my own and I never should have gotten Jade involved," I said, and waited for Tones to scream at me, maybe even throw me in jail for the night; just to teach me a lesson.

"Right now, I'm just glad you're alright. You guys could have been killed. If it wasn't for your friend here . . . Ahh . . . Violet."

"Enchanté." Fuchsia appeared at my Dad's side and he just looked at her, confused, for a moment. "That's Fuchsia. Fuchsia Darling, at your service."

"Yes, sorry. Fuchsia. She called in with the address." Tones sounded like he was still in utter disbelief at what was happening.

Fuchsia gave his shoulder a consoling little pat and he slowly scooted away from her, completely out of his realm of comfort.

"Does this mean you're not mad?" Jade asked.

"Nice try, kid. You're grounded . . . until your thirty-five," Tones said to Jade, before pointing his finger in my face. "And you . . . I'll deal with you later. You're gonna get yourself killed one of these days."

"Can I get some love?" Matty asked, as he joined in on the group bear hug and threw his long arms around us. Jade and I took a few minutes to explain exactly what happened tonight, while Tones, Matty, and Fuchsia listened with growing curiosity.

"Wait a minute . . ." Tones interrupted Jade. "What do you mean, you kissed him?" My dad ran his fingers through his salt and pepper hair and his complexion turned beet red.

"There's more." I interrupted my Dad this time, trying to deflect attention from the whole kissing thing. "I gouged his eyeball out with my thumb," I said, with a straight face.

"Atta girl! I taught you well." Tones seemed pleased, and then he was back to business as usual. "So essentially, you're telling me that we're looking for a pervert with a missing eye and a scar? Can you give me any more details? Facial characteristics, anything?" Tones asked incredulously, and we left out the part about the Taser gun. After listening to my Dad give us the third degree, he eventually calmed himself down to a manageable level.

"What am I gonna do with you two knuckleheads, huh?" he asked. "Just so we're clear, the only reason I'm not mad is because you're safe. Now, if only you could have actually caught the guy too . . ." Tones teased us.

"I'm starving. Can we stop by Luigi's on the way home?" Jade asked, as if nothing had ever happened. "Well, maybe we should let Marley shower first. Wipe the guts off her hands and all."

Because there really wasn't any paperwork for the police to fill out at the scene, we got out of there relatively quickly. Within an hour, I was freshly showered. Jade and I both changed into oversized sweatshirts and jeans, feeling cozy out of our hooker-wear. Tones, Matty, Jade, Fuchsia, and I had all just ordered two pizzas.

"Marley, I almost forgot. A Mark Monroe from ABC news called me. He was trying to find a way to get in touch with you."

"I thought we agreed that I wasn't going to give out any more interviews on the Cummings murder case?"

"We did. That's not what this call was about." He looked at me with a peculiar twinkle in his eye that told me he was about to tell something good. "He wants to hire you, you know, for a job in television."

"Come on. Is this a joke? Television? Seriously?" I scratched my chin and mulled over the magnitude of Tones's words. "But . . . this is what I'm going to school for. Nobody gets this kind of opportunity when they're still *in* school."

“Except you,” Jade said, smiling.

“Here, I wrote down his name and number for you. He said he wants you come into the station and get started right away.”

CHAPTER 22

Roughly one week after my cornfield adventure, I was frantically trying to catch up on the exorbitant amount of homework and writing I had let slide to the waste side over the last couple of weeks. Things seemed to be a bit calmer this week. I had a soothing feeling of closure, knowing that I had partially blinded the Boogeyman and found the source of the haunting at the hotel. The Boogeyman had still not been found and arrested by authorities. However, no other women had been reported killed or assaulted in Greenbriar since that night; which was cause enough for celebration. Maybe I had just scared him enough to make him stop for a while, or even permanently.

There had been no further rumors of ghost sightings at the Brass Lantern Inn since the discovery of the body in the pond. This was a huge relief and it made me feel good to know that I helped to give Ryan Duff a little peace of mind regarding his sister. My dad was still waiting on word from the coroner's office to find out exactly who the remains belonged to. But, I already knew . . . they *were* Addy's bones.

In other news, Rose had been home for well over a week now. Her brother, Jeff Daily, drove in from Kansas City, Missouri to help her out. I could only assume that's who she was asking for, the night I stood next to her hospital bed and she kept muttering *'Eff.'* She had pretty much already made a full recovery and started back at school this morning. She still had a few scrapes and bruises but they had swiftly faded into putrid shades of yellow and green.

She said she didn't remember much about being attacked. She told me the last thing that she remembered was being pulled over by a police car and the 'officer' demanded she get out of the car, which she refused to do, insisting that she had done nothing wrong. That's when he became angry and beat her up.

I had my first official interview, if you want to call it that, at WKKP Television this morning. They immediately offered me a part-time position as a reporter—of sorts. They had read my articles and had been impressed with the way I conducted my interviews on national television, in the aftermath of the Cummings murder. WKKP's General Manager, Gene Fairbanks, admitted that he had essentially created a position for me on their team. I was assured by both my Dad and by Doc Warner that this was a sage career move. I was already envisioning all the cute outfits and accessories I would wear on air.

I was at the school coffee shop, preparing for a test in abnormal psych with my study group, when my cell rang. The caller ID displayed the name: Matty.

"What's up, Bro?" I answered the phone and walked away from the table to avoid disturbing the group.

"Ohhh, just calling to gloat . . ."

"Gloat?" I asked him suspiciously, already sensing something was awry. "Well, by all means, don't let me keep you from *gloating*."

"DNA testing just came back on the bones from the pond."

"And . . ." I found Matty's patronizing tone highly irritating, which I knew was his intention.

"And, I know who the remains belong to," he responded, drawing out the suspense just a little longer.

"Tell me!"

"They belonged to one Edward Russell Whitmore."

"Huh? No, that can't be right . . . Come on."

"I'm dead serious." Matty just realized the irony of his last statement and chuckled to himself. I could picture him sitting in his office filled with sports memorabilia from the Chicago Cubs, Bears, and Blackhawks teams. He had a tendency to scratch the back of his head now and then, when he spoke. Even though he was in his late forties, most would have assumed mid-twenties. His boyish looks gave him a sort of innocent quality, endearing people to him. "Edward Russell Whitmore . . ."

"It's just that I thought the bones belonged to Addy *Duff* Whitmore, the wife. I just didn't see that as a variable. It blows my whole theory."

"Remind me again, what theory was that?"

“Well, it’s a long story, but essentially, I speculated that Addy couldn’t swim and for whatever reason, her husband drowned her in the pond. Addy is the ghost at the Brass Lantern Inn, so naturally I assumed the bones were Addy’s.”

“Yes, naturally.” Matty never missed an opportunity to mock me. “I won’t ask how you came to that conclusion . . .” Matty chuckled to himself again then sighed. “Well, Sherlock, you can’t win ‘em all.”

I remained silent on my end of the line. For once, I didn’t know what to say.

“Hey, look on the bright side: There haven’t been any more ghost sightings . . . I mean . . . at the hotel. Right?”

“That’s true. I just don’t understand. What does this mean? That Addy was the killer? That she killed her husband? Or, a third person could have killed them both and gotten away with it. There are too many open-ended questions here. I mean, clearly Addy is dead too. She’s the one haunting the place, not Russell whatever the hell his name is . . . Was.”

“It was Edward Russell Whitmore . . . beside the point . . . I get it. Marley, this is a matter for the professionals, now. Let us do our jobs. You just sit there and look pretty.”

CHAPTER 23

I returned home from my morning jog to see a man standing at my door holding a rather long rectangular box with a big red bow on the top of it. I assumed the black Prius parked in my driveway belonged to him. There was a sign on the driver's side door that read 'X-press Couriers.'

"Can I help you?" I asked the short man, a septuagenarian with white hair that matched the white stripe in his black track suit.

"Are you, erm . . . Miss Parker?" The elderly man looked down at his notes to double check my name.

"That's me." I looked down at the beautifully wrapped box, desperately hoping it was meant for me.

"Can you sign here for me?" he asked, in a rushed tone, as he handed me a pen and a receipt of sorts. After I signed my name, the man handed me the box, told me to have a nice day, and took off in a hurry.

I didn't waste a moment before unwrapping the mysterious box. I took a seat on my front porch and set my headphones and my sunglasses next to me. I opened the ivory envelope and removed the matching notecard. It was Rob's personal stationary. I could tell because it had his full name embossed on the bottom in an elegant black typeset, 'Robert L. Cummings, Jr.' I recognized Rob's childish handwriting instantly: *'Let's start over. Meet me tonight, Hotel Raven, 7PM. Wear this and let me prove how crazy I am about you.*

Slowly and carefully, I opened the box. I gently unfolded the silver tissue paper that was wrapped around the prettiest dress I had ever seen. It was bright white, spaghetti strapped, with a low cut and fitted bodice. It was gathered around the waist and long, hitting me at the ankles. I picked it up, letting the box fall to the ground, and I held it up to my body. It was absolutely gorgeous. I felt butterflies in my stomach. My face blushed at the thought of Rob selecting this dress at a designer dress shop, with me in mind. I knew this very moment was one I would remember for years to come. It was highly unlikely anything like this would ever happen to me again, so I relished every second of opening such a gift.

I decided to meet Rob at the Hotel Raven. I had been mentally preparing myself for this for a long time now. I guess a part of me always knew that this day would come. I just didn't realize it would be quite this grand of a gesture on Rob's behalf: the gorgeous white gown he had sent over, the fetching invite, and no doubt a romantic and glamorous evening in store.

I asked Jade to come over and help me get dolled up for my big night. My hands were far too shaky to apply my eye makeup, so Jade had to take over. I studied her rounded face as she leaned in closer and carefully applied the charcoal liner to my lash lines with one long steady swoop of her hand, and as she gently brushed on multiple layers of pitch black mascara. Her doll-like features gave her a dreamy appearance: her big, oval-shaped, jade colored eyes surrounded by a thick dark lashes, her high cheek bones and full sweetheart shaped lips, a prominent endowment passed down to her from our paternal heritage. She never fully realized the extent of her beauty, which somehow made her even prettier.

"Do you know why mom named you Jade?" I asked her curiously, as she was blowing at my lashes and batting them with her hands.

"Mmm, not really. I just assumed maybe we had a great aunt Jade somewhere."

"No, she named you Jade because of the color of your eyes."

Jade thought about that for a minute and looked pleased. "I always wondered how she chose my name." She smiled to herself at the thought of our mother seeing her for the first time and selecting a name for the screaming newborn she held in her arms. "So, what are you going to talk about? I mean, what is left to say to each other?" The sound of Jade's morbid curiosity cut through the small space of air between us.

"I have no idea, Jade. I haven't thought that far ahead." My voice sounded defeated and tired. "If I did, my head might explode."

"Can I borrow the dress when you're done with it?"

"It's all yours."

I pulled into the front entrance at the Hotel Raven at seven o'clock sharp. I decided to drive myself because I needed to be in control of this situation and I had to have the freedom to leave if things got uncomfortable . . . or if they got a little too comfortable.

The hotel was independently owned by the Cummings family and had been a mainstay in the town of Greenbriar ever since I could remember. It was somewhat modest in size compared to the other handful of hotels in town but what it lacked in size, it made for in charm. It wasn't your typical cookie cutter hotel; it was elegant and dreamy, somewhere special occasions should be celebrated. Reservations for both the hotel suites and the restaurant inside were required months ahead of time. The last time I'd been there was for my Sweet Sixteen birthday party.

I walked through the inviting entryway, taking a look around. It was just as I remembered it, except now I noticed the similarities in the hotel décor and the décor in the Cummings estate, Manor Hill, which was now nothing but a heaping pile of ashes. The colors were all shades of lush greens, velvety grays, and gilded accents. Long, heavy drapes spilled onto the floor like puddles and the fanciest crystal chandeliers I had ever seen hung from the vaulted ceilings, making everything sparkle.

I took the elevator up to the second floor. As the elevator began to open, I suddenly felt like I had just dove head first into an icy pool of anxiety and I felt an overwhelming urge to leave. Just leave this mess behind once and for all, Rob especially. What was left to say? The doors opened and I saw a man standing in front of the elevator with his back turned to me. The audible ding of the doors as they opened caused him to turn toward me. Good Lord, help me . . . he was *so hot.* The second our eyes met, I knew I wasn't going anywhere. My inner fears began to ebb, replaced with a warm energetic sensation. For tonight, this is where I belonged. Neither one of us spoke a word; we only studied each other, taking in every detail, every line, every wayward freckle or dimple, every trace of emotion that the other's expression might convey.

It felt like we were getting to know each other in a different way this time. Not as the spoiled, rich playboy and the ditzy co-ed, but as two people who had experienced a tragedy and survived it together. The playing field had, without a doubt, been leveled slightly and now he was forever in my debt. After all, I had saved his life and my own. I had saved the day, solved the mystery, and became a semi-famous journalist overnight because of it. He had lost his father, his home, and his family name would forever be tarnished, and he was all alone. Sure, he had inherited his family's fortune, but what good was money without happiness?

"Hi," I said, my voice unsteady and shaky.

"You look . . ." Rob hesitated, in search of the perfect words. "Beautiful. You are beautiful." He spoke the words slowly, without a trace of pretention or sarcasm, like his usual tone precluded. He sounded different to me, almost timid.

I couldn't help but smile, pleased with his newfound submissiveness. "Well, I suppose I do look rather fetching in this dress that probably costs as much a semester of tuition at G.U.," I teased, as I attempted to lighten the mood ever so slightly.

"No, no. It's not the dress, it's just you. You're radiant." He stared at me for another moment longer and I didn't look away. After what felt like a lapse in time and space, he held out his hand for me to take. "Worth every penny," he whispered in my ear, and squeezed me in closer to his body as he led me through the second floor lobby, to the restaurant.

We were seated at a small round table directly in the center of the crowded restaurant. It felt like the music stopped when we walked in. Everyone was staring, whispering, gossiping about the couple who had been plastered all over the news. The kids that made national headlines, the girl who solved the murder of her mother and then fell in love with the son of the man who killed her, before saving his life. I must admit, I'd probably be talking about us too. We were not exactly the typical love story and besides, I kind of liked the attention.

The waiter came by to take our drink orders and without hesitating, Rob ordered a water. I ordered the same and glanced at Rob curiously. "What happened to your fancy Scotch or whiskey or whatever it was?"

"I quit drinking." He leaned in closer to the table and took a quick glance around at the eavesdropping patrons, dining in his establishment. "Looking back . . ." He hesitated and rubbed his fingertips together. He lowered his voice before continuing, "Well, let's just say, I didn't very much like who I was. That is to say, when

I drank. Well, altogether. I was turning into my Dad." He shook his head a little, as if warding off a cold chill. "So I gave it up. I'm a different person now."

"A different person?" I tried not to laugh out loud, "Rob, it's only been . . . a month, or so?" I replied skeptically, making it clear that I was also a different person. That I had also changed and I was not going to just buy whatever load of shit he was throwing my way. I tilted my chin down and stared at him curiously.

"What? I'm telling you. I've changed. I saw my life flash before my eyes that night. I mean, I really thought that was it for me. Ya know? Death by fire," he said, in a surprisingly self-effacing manner. "I remember the last thing that crossed my mind. I thought: What I have done with my life? What legacy have I left behind? Nothing. I contributed nothing to this planet, merely leaving it as I found it. Perhaps, a little worse. I don't know. I suppose facing death forces a person to reevaluate their life."

"Well, maybe you're alive right now for a reason. Maybe, you need to leave Greenbriar. Just go travel. Go on a missionary trip, join the Peace Corps, or finish law school. The world is your oyster."

"Funny you should say that. I did travel. I spent this last month just cruising through Europe. The Louvre in Paris, the Vatican in Rome, mountain biking through the Swiss Alps, just marveling at the architecture in Prague. I even made it over to Spain for the ninth time in my life. I guess you could call it soul searching."

"I had a feeling that's what you were up to. Especially, since you didn't call—" Suddenly, I had forgotten how to play it cool. If he was going to be real, then so was I.

Rob interrupted me before I could finish my thought. "Marley, I'm sorry. I didn't know what to say. You must understand that. I mean, put yourself in my shoes. You have no idea how I feel. I feel so guilty, so awful about what happened to you and your family. Knowing that it was my father who was responsible . . ." He shook his head in utter disgust. His pallor swiftly became paler as his blue eyes wandered across the room and away from me, for the first time since we had sat down.

"Rob, don't. I don't want to talk about that." I held up my hand, in a gesture that conveyed, '*stop, my mother is off limits . . . right now.*' I would not let her be reduced to the source of polite dinner conversation; she was someone who deserved more. There was a time and a place to tell him all about my mother and now was not it. "It has nothing to do with you. I realize that now. You and your dad are two different people. You can't be held responsible for his actions."

"You mean . . . you don't hate me?" He seemed relieved.

"Hate you? No. I don't hate you and I've never blamed *you* for anything either. I'll admit that it bothers me a little; it's bizarre." I took a deep breath, unsure of the words I wanted to use to convey something so important. "Rob, do you really think I would have saved your life if I blamed you for my mother's death?"

He mulled that last question over before answering, "Yes, actually. I think you would have saved me anyway, because that's just the kind of person you are."

"Okay, well. I guess you're right about that, but you're not off the hook that easily. If you're truly sorry, you have to prove it," I said, part teasing and the other part serious. "And, I don't mean prove it by buying me a fancy dress or another fancy car. Just . . . be real."

"Be real, huh?" he asked, rubbing his chin now, clearly deep in thought, calculating how he would do just that. "Alright . . . Marley. I love you," he blurted, without warning. His words hung in the air between us like a cloud.

My eyeballs nearly fell out of my skull and rolled out across the table. Perhaps I had misheard.

"Huh?" I asked stupidly, staring at him blankly. Unable to move, all I could do was try to keep my mouth from gaping wide open. Then I watched as Rob stood up, got out of his seat, walked around the small table, and knelt down in front of me. Whatever was happening, I was *not* prepared for.

Rob bent down, grabbed both of my hands, and said, "You heard me. I love you." He made no attempt to lower his voice or care about who might be overhearing this emotional declaration. In fact, it was almost the opposite, like he wanted to announce it to anyone within earshot of us. Then, he said it again, this time nearly shouting the words, "I'm in love with you, Marley Parker!" He leaned in to kiss me with an open, eager mouth. "I want to be with you," he whispered this time. "You're all I think about."

At this point, I felt like I was the star of a reality show and I was secretly praying that Rob wasn't going to do something completely stupid, like propose marriage. I was blushing, equal parts embarrassed and well . . . *happy*. I wasn't expecting any of this. I was just hoping for a quiet night, just the two of us, in a cozy nook somewhere, hashing things out.

But as far as Rob was concerned, the words cozy and nook were not part of his vocabulary. I couldn't help but smile and what girl wouldn't smile at such flattery. It was more like an involuntary reflex. He was quite obviously repentant for disappearing, without calling. I had no real reason not to believe his story about wanting to find himself and change his ways. Even more so, I wanted to believe him. So I let him kiss me again and I reciprocated this time.

I listened and even laughed a little at the cat calls and whistles from the surrounding patrons who had overheard our little side show. I pulled my face away, breaking off the kiss and shyly rested my head against his chest, embarrassed. Then, without warning, Rob scooped me up into his arms like I was a ragdoll, a gesture only a man like Rob could perfectly execute and make look sensational, like something right out of an old-fashioned black and white movie. He carried me over to the dance floor with ease, both of us laughing mischievously along the way. After all, he did own the hotel, which allowed him to do or say anything he wanted without any repercussions. We danced slowly and fell into each other's arms comfortably, without any awkwardness. It felt natural, like slipping into a warm bubble bath. The song playing was easily one of the prettiest, most haunting songs I had ever heard; it sounded like Coldplay.

Rob kissed me again and I pulled away slowly. I wanted to look at his face, study him, and make sure he was serious about what he had said. There was still an awful lot that I was unsure about. This man was still a mystery to me.

"What?" he asked, grinning.

"I just can't believe this is really happening. I feel like Cinderella."

After a bit of dancing and an exchange of longing gazes, we returned to our table, hand in hand. While we waited for our food, we had so much to talk about, it felt like we were racing to see who could fill the other in the fastest. Rob talked a lot about his travels and a little about his family: about his hatred for his father and how he had disliked him his whole life. He explained that he always had an unsettled feeling about him, that he was never fully at ease in his presence, but never quite understood why. Now, he understood why: Subconsciously, he had always felt that way because his dad was guilty of such a heinous crime that even as a young child, he could sense something was off. He briefly brought up his mother and informed me that she had recently become engaged to her much younger boyfriend of only six months. He also explained that the girl he was with at Ryan's party was just an old friend that he had just bumped into that night.

Just before our entrees arrived, Rob excused himself to use the restroom. While he was gone, the waiter delivered two plates with cheeseburgers, accompanied by heaping piles of French fries. I instinctively laughed aloud at Rob's gesture, which I found to be completely adorable, not to mention completely atypical for him. He was all about the glam: the shiniest, the brightest, and the best of everything.

I stared at the burger longingly, as I debated if I should just go for it and eat the whole thing or if I should be a lady and just take a few nibbles off the side. Tricky call. I took a sweeping glance around the room as I admired the older couple on the dance floor, the dim lighting from the candles, and the rather romantic ambiance. I noticed a larger group of eight or so people, just a few tables in front of me. They all seemed to be engrossed in a joke that was being told by the white-haired man seated at the head of the table, then simultaneously broke out into a forced sort of laughter. As my eyes moved quickly across the faces, I backtracked on the last face I saw. Could it be?

Yes, it was. It was Dr. John Wright. Our eyes met and I quickly looked away, embarrassed for staring. I could still feel his gaze, so I brought my eyes back up to meet his again and he gave a little wave and smiled politely. Oh god, he probably witnessed Rob's declaration of love. I took a deep breath and glanced at my wrist watch. Rob had been gone for over five minutes now. Where was he? Our food was starting to get cold. Another five minutes went by and I was passing the time by checking my friend's status updates on my social media networks. I then busied myself by reading some unopened emails. Finally, after another five minutes passed, I sent him a text message asking if everything was alright. I waited impatiently for his response. Nothing. I felt the familiar ebb of fear begin to rise from my midline. Where was he? It had been at least fifteen minutes since he had left. I couldn't help but worry and it must have come across on my face. Just as I was about to get on the Nordstrom app, I heard a man's voice at my side.

"Chin up princess or else the crown falls down."

I looked up from my phone to see Dr. John Wright standing next to my table, looking adorable in a dark grey suit, his brown hair wavy hair tousled as usual. "Hello, John, or I guess I should say, Dr. Wright, since, technically you were the last doctor to treat me." I was babbling to disguise my unease with the current situation.

"Please, call me John," he said, with a dismissive little flitter of his hand and smiled at me.

"Ok, John it is."

"So, I didn't realize you had a boyfriend. I mean, I assume he's your boyfriend. The guy's obviously crazy about you."

"Ha . . . we're in a grey area. I don't know if boyfriend is the right word. More like reuniting with an old flame, I guess you could say. That's probably not accurate either. I don't think there's a name for what you would call us." I continued to ramble, followed by a nervous laugh.

"Wasn't that the guy you saved from the fire?" I could see him connecting the dots in his mind. "Come to think of it, doesn't he own this hotel?" Before I could interject with some inane comment, Dr. John Wright sighed and said, "Well, whatever he is . . . he's a lucky guy." He paused, smiling with his eyes. "I'm here for a resident dinner, actually. It's clearly not as much fun as you're having."

"I don't know about that. Actually, I think my date might have left me for some more interesting company. He seems to have pulled the ol' disappearing act on me," I said, confused, and took another sip of my water.

"Well, you can come join us if you like. We would probably bore you but there's an extra seat . . ."

"Oh, no. Thank you but I couldn't. I mean, I probably just misunderstood him. I'm sure he's just on the phone or something," I lied. "Thank you though. Maybe another time." The words sounded more aggressive than I had intended. In reality, I was trying to deflect any attention away from the rather embarrassing situation that was arising.

I looked down at my watch: It was now a total of twenty-five minutes that Rob had been gone and still no response to my text. *That's it,* I decided. *It's best to leave. How stupid could I be to have trusted him, to think that he was a changed man?* He probably met another girl on his way to the bathroom and was already cheating on me. Feeling more and more disgusted with each passing second, I reached for my bag, stood up, and delicately placed my napkin on the table, next to the plates of uneaten food.

I looked across the room at John Wright and he looked almost hopeful, ready for me to occupy the empty seat next to his. I gave him a dismissive little wave along with my best smile and sauntered off, fully conscious of his eyes still on me. Normally, the idea of spending an evening with him would excite me beyond words, but not tonight. Tonight my heart didn't belong to me at all.

As I walked out into the brisk evening, I pulled my pashmina tighter around me. I looked up at the stars to see an expansive moon that hung low in the sky. It was quiet, peaceful. I forced myself to look forward, hastily picking up my pace until I was sprinting through the vast parking lot in my high heels. Never again would I fall for his charms. I felt so incredibly stupid. Without warning, hot tears stung my eyes and rolled down my cheeks. I unlocked my car and conscientiously climbed in, careful not to rip the gorgeous white fabric on the designer dress—the gift that I should have never accepted. It was a beautiful shining symbol of a relationship that was doomed from the start, another lapse in judgment from the trusting, naïve Marley.

I turned the key in the ignition and a familiar old rock song blared powerfully from the speakers, something about a *'stranglehold.'* I didn't care; it helped drown out my steady stream of despondent thoughts. I glanced in the rearview mirror and used the back of my hands to wipe away the dripping streaks of black mascara. I pushed a button that lowered the heavy convertible top, impatiently waiting for it to lower when I saw *it*. The white envelope, with my name written across the middle in a meticulous script.

I sat frozen in my seat for a moment and staring at it. Unsure I wanted to see what was inside. Slowly, I put the car back into park, opened my door, and carefully plucked out the envelope. Fearful of whatever lies and excuses I was about to endure, I tore open the envelope, slowly unfolded the letter and began to read the carefully typed script.

'Blood is red.
Veins are blue.
The bottom of the lake is where they will find you.'

That's when I noticed the warmth slowly begin to creep down my arms. Then I felt it: White pain, a dull ache that split through me. I studied the letter alarmingly as if it would leech itself onto my face and suffocate me. I flipped it over, quickly examining the back. There were sharp blades of some sort stuck to the back of the letter--Razor blades. The letter fell from my hands…My hands. They looked like they had been sliced open. Deep red droplets of blood began to form stains down the front of my white gown, like a rain shower of blood. The electrifying sounds of my screams echoed throughout the sleepy town.

CHAPTER 24

I made it back home from the hotel in one piece and resisted the urge to call for help, from both my Dad and from 911. I wasn't quite sure what I would say and I didn't want my Dad to panic. I suppose there was no *real* emergency anyway. My hands were cut deeply from the razor blades but I wasn't sure if stitches were totally necessary. The minute I stepped inside my house, I threw away the blood-soaked napkins that I had been gripping tightly in my hands to control the bleeding. I walked over to the sink and winced as I held my hands under the cold running water. Once the wounds were clean and the blood slowed, I grabbed a kitchen towel and applied more pressure to the cuts.

My mind wandered, reflecting on everything that had just happened: the horrifying letter, the sensation of my hands being sliced open, and the sound of Rob's voice as he announced his love for me. It resounded in my head. Over and over, I kept seeing his face in front of mine, not giving a damn who heard. "*All of this could be yours . . .*" If he loved me so much, why did he just leave me there? I felt like a fool . . . no . . . *I feel like a fool. Every time I let my guard down around him, he just proves himself to be an untrustworthy ass all over again.*

I mean, who does that? There was only so much I could let myself live with, when it came to a potential partner. Rob already had quite the list of miscreant character flaws, so I guess I could add disappearing acts to that list too. My bloodshot eyes, red from crying, drifted down from the night sky and over the rippling water. *That's when I saw it.* It was red and it glistened in the moonlight. It looked like it was tied to a light post on my boat dock. A single red balloon. It had to be filled with helium, the way it floated in the air. *How odd.*

Before I thought anything through, I walked out the double doors off of my kitchen and made my way down the back yard, until I reached the dock. I hardly ever used the dock, especially this time of year. The night air was so quiet; no one else was outside or on the water. I slowly approached the balloon, as if it might attack me in some way.

How in the hell did this get here? What was this all about? As I came in closer, I saw that something had been written on it, with a black marker. Oh, no. Another note from the Boogeyman, perhaps? Before I reached for the balloon, I took another look around me, making sure this wasn't some kind of a trap. There was nothing, no sound, no one in sight. Only the steady sounds of the ebb and flow from the ripples in the lake. I tried to hold the balloon steady in my hand, so I could read the wording but my hands were shaking so much, it was a challenge.

'You'll never know when I might find you,

stabbing, choking, creeping up behind you.
You better start running and pray that they find me.
When you forget to look, that's when I'll be coming.'

Before my brain could even process the severity of the message, I saw something or someone out of my peripheral vision.

It all happened so fast. He leaped from the inside the speed boat and onto the boat dock, landing right in front of me. He must have been hiding in the boat the entire time, hunched down in the darkness. I already knew it was the Boogeyman, even before I noticed that he was missing an eye. The fear that aroused deep within me from the sight of his hideous face caused me to involuntarily vomit a little in my mouth.

Suddenly, he grabbed hold of my neck and began to choke me. He started to drag me to the edge of the dock, preparing to throw me in and ultimately drown me.

I tried to fight back but it was useless. I remembered how resistant he was to my all of my attacks, that night in the cornfields. I wasn't physically able to say anything to try and talk him out of it because I was choking and fading fast. I felt my head get light and everything started to fade in the distance.

I heard a loud booming sound and his grip loosened, plunging me directly into the lake. The icy water shocked my system and I came to the surface, gasping and wheezing. My eyes frantically searched for the Boogeyman and for the source of the loud boom I had just heard seconds before he dropped me in the water. I coughed and flailed my arms like a helpless baby bird who had fallen from its nest. I was in a state of complete and utter shock. What was happening? I needed help. Help. I had to scream for help.

"HELP! SOMEBODY HELP ME!" My pathetic screams fell flat and short. It seemed like a physical impossibility to raise my voice any louder. "HELP!" I tried to scream again but my voice only came out in a sort of raspy whisper.

I pulled myself out of the water and back onto the dock. At my feet, there he was. Charles Skinner lay face down on my dock, yelping in pain. Seconds later, I saw someone in the distance, running over to us.

"MARLEY! Are you okay?" A man's yell sliced through the night air like a chainsaw, instantly zapping me out of my dream like trance. It was Ryan Duff, holding a formidable looking gun. I couldn't tell what kind of gun, but there was some type of scope resting on the top and a red laser beam.

"I'm . . . I'm fine," I stuttered, both freezing and horrified. I still wasn't fully processing the sequence of events that had just unfolded.

"Is he dead? Did I kill the bastard?" Ryan yelled as he rushed over to the dock. "Look away!" he instructed with all of the authority and confidence of a soldier in battle.

I did as I was told and the deafening blast of a second gunshot boomed loudly. I opened my eyes and looked down to see Charles Skinner now with two bullet holes through his back, finally silent and lifeless.

"He's dead now," Ryan said, quite pleased with himself.

I couldn't believe it. Skinner was dead and I was alive. Ryan had saved me. Maybe he really was my guardian angel. Now this mess was over, but what about Rob? I was worried that Rob somehow had gotten caught up in all of this. What if Charles Skinner had attacked him or killed him? Rob could be in the middle of nowhere by now, or even at the bottom of the lake. Now that the Boogeyman was dead, I might never know for sure.

EPILOGUE

My head was throbbing. *What the hell just happened? Where am I?* I tried to open my eyes but my lids felt so unbelievably heavy. The pain in my side was too intense to tolerate. It was dark and the cold air reeked of gasoline . . . motor oil. I stretched out my legs, only to feel a hard barrier under my feet. I shoved out my feet again, harder this time. Nothing but a hard, metal wall of sorts under my feet. My hands were constrained, so calling for help from my cell was out of the question. I forced my eyes open--nothing but blackness all around me. It felt like I was inside of a casket.

Excruciating shards of pain raged through me especially, on my face. My memories quickly began to rush back. That's right…he had slashed up my face. It hurt like hell and if I survive this night, there was no question that my appearance would forever be altered. The dampness I felt wasn't water but blood. I forgot that I was covered in it. Then I felt movement, rattling . . . I was being taken somewhere. That crazy freak had me tied up in the trunk of his car.

"Get me out of here!" I yelled, kicking the sides of the car's trunk so hard the metal was denting. "Stop the car asshole!" I yelled until my voice came out in raspy moans.

All I could think about was Marley. Was she alright? Did he have her? "Marley!" Where was she? Was she in the car? Was she still alive? Now, the panic had officially set in. "Marley! Marley! Where are you?" I kept yelling until my voice was gone, my eyelids felt heavy, and the blackness slowly surrounded me like an old friend.